The Blood Runs Deep

Jim and Aaron were brothers brought up on the same plantation. However, Jim was dark-skinned and Aaron was white and this created a chasm between them that widened when Jim ran off to fight in the Civil War.

After the war, and on the run from the army and hostile Comanches, Jim rides into Texas seeking his mother. But, here, fate unites the two brothers in pursuit of renegades Red Bill, an adversary from Jim's war days.

Once again, Jim and Aaron's relationship is tested. Does their shared blood count?

For Mr Peter Henry Taylor
always a hero to his
wife and son

The Blood Runs Deep

Peter Taylor

A Black Horse Western

ROBERT HALE · LONDON

Typeset by
Derek Doyle & Associates, Shaw Heath.
Printed and bound in Great Britain by
Antony Rowe Limited, Wiltshire

1

Jim Macleod lifted his arm and wiped the grime from his black, sweat-streaked face. He stole a glance at his friend, Private Hooker, could see the strain of battle etched into his features as he crouched behind the light artillery gun. In the same second, another sniper's bullet kicked up dirt a yard away and in reflex action the two men bunched closer together. Macleod saw Hooker's eyes widen and dart everywhere in the vain hope that there was somewhere to run. Then, in a moment of mutual understanding that all was lost, his eyes met Macleod's.

'We're done for!' Macleod voiced it like a curse.

His words were scarcely spoken when the sounds of the battle started to die away. The enemy snipers stopped firing and Hooker took advantage of that respite to raise his eyes above the gun and scan the surrounding knolls from which the Confederate marksmen had peppered them. Macleod did the same. Momentarily, before they ducked down again, he registered the carnage in front of him, the soldiers of the 2nd US light artillery (coloured) decimated by the enemy fire and, through the wreaths of smoke, a white flag waving.

Hooker turned to Macleod, tears of frustration in his eyes. He said dolefully:

'Major Bradford's put up the white flag.'

Macleod sighed. 'It's going to be a Confederate prison for you and me for the rest of the war.'

'Like being a slave again,' Hooker grunted disconsolately, his shoulders hunching forward.

'Got to hope the Union win this war quick,' Macleod said, staring far off. ' 'Cos I don't suppose they'll treat us ex-slaves too well.'

He raised himself to look over the gun. The survivors were moving cautiously out from behind the guns, like men entering unknown territory, unsure of everything, as though they couldn't believe the fusillade had finally ended. He felt sadness but it was tempered with pride, pride that coloured men had fought so bravely against overwhelming odds, that their valiant efforts here at Fort Pillow would be remembered.

'Least, maybe you'll never have to kill anyone again, Hooker,' he said, sitting again. 'It was never easy for you, was it, being religious and all?'

Hooker spat. 'Only reason I'm here is so the brothers and sisters can be freed when this is over. Didn't never intend ending up in a Confederate prison though. Had enough of the South's contempt.'

'Well, you've done your bit for the cause. A man can only see so much dying.'

Simultaneously, they glanced at their companion

lying a few feet off. A Yankee bullet had torn out his throat and the flies were already feasting. Hooker leaned over the body, swiped at them angrily and started to unbutton the man's tunic.

'What in the hell you doing, Hooker?'

Hooker scooped up the cap that lay discarded in the dust and threw it at him. He finished pulling off the tunic and passed it over.

'Put 'em on,' he commanded. 'Those boys in grey see you're not properly joined up, no telling what they might do.'

'Never thought of that,' Macleod said, doing as he was told. As always, in the heat of battle, he'd forgotten he was just a teamster who looked after the horses and supplies. It was a vital job, one he'd taken when, as a runaway, he'd bumped into the black troopers. He'd fled the plantation to be part of the war and, though he hadn't been obliged to, he'd always fought alongside his coloured friends in the thick of the action.

'We ready?' Hooker said when he was done.

'Suppose,' Macleod muttered.

They stood up, stepped out reluctantly from behind the gun. With the other scattered survivors, they watched a cluster of cavalrymen, Nathan Bedford's finest, riding into the inner redoubt with the confident air of victors.

Hooker spat, narrowed his eyes warily.

'The masters are back for us.'

A hundred yards away from the vanquished men, without slackening pace, the riders began split up, came as individuals towards the weary coloured troops. Macleod felt his stomach churn. Something not quite right here. The horsemen were coming too fast. More than just the exhilaration of victory was driving them on. But he was helpless to do anything about it now except wait with foreboding.

Almost before they knew it one of the riders was upon them, reining in his horse which rose up and kicked the air with its front feet not a yard from them, filling their vision. Steam poured from its nostrils and, as it snorted, black stones of eyes rolled wildly in its white face. The Confederate rider steadied it down and swept off his hat to reveal a shock of red hair. Beneath his low forehead, small eyes set in a heavily freckled face looked down at them. His lips were set too tightly, giving the impression he was a man who found it difficult to hold on to his spite.

'Behold a pale horse,' Macleod said, quoting Revelation.

Private Hooker added, only louder: 'And the name of him who sits up on it is—'

At that moment, somewhere beyond the horseman they heard a scream, then another.

'What's happening?' Hooker yelled.

Off to their left, a tall Negro staggered into their vision, fell headlong into the dust. On their other side, a horseman chased a Negro down and shot him in the head.

'Wish you'd stayed where you belonged now, uh!' The redhead drew his sword from its scabbard as he spoke. 'Better in the fields picking cotton, I'd say. Best say your prayers, boys, 'cos today there'll be an example set for all your kind.'

Disbelieving, neither Macleod nor Hooker moved as the horseman swung the sword above his head, edged his mount a step towards them. In a blur of movement the weapon started on a downward arc towards Macleod. He started backwards to avoid the slashing blade but, with one long scream of defiance, Hooker stepped between him and the Confederate to take the full force of the blow on his arm.

The shock of the unexpected attack caused Macleod to stumble. As he fell, he heard Hooker's agonized cry. When he looked up his friend's arm was hanging off and a red torrent of blood was spurting from it. Rage filling his world, obliterating everything but the man who had perpetrated that horrific butchery, he rose again and started to advance towards the Confederate.

Before he could reach him the redhead was swinging the sword ready to strike Hooker again. Helpless to prevent it, Macleod screamed as the blade descended once again with a practised perfection.

Time seemed to slow as the honed edge sliced into Hooker's neck, cut smoothly through it to emerge at the other side. His head remained poised on his shoulders for what seemed for ever. Then, like a fruit ripe for falling, it slid off its axis, toppled though the air, hit the ground and bounced against Macleod's legs. The decapitated body buckled at the knees and slumped forward to land under the horse's hoofs. Macleod, caught mid-stride, froze on the spot, his own head a maelstrom of swirling emotions as he struggled to comprehend what had just happened to his friend whose eyes were staring grotesquely up at him from that severed head.

Jim recovered his senses just enough to avoid the next downward slash of the sword which was intended to decapitate him. A third time the sword rose. Jim saw the bloodlust in the redhead's small eyes but this time he was ready and went under the striking arm, grasped it with both hands, pulling downwards with all the strength he could muster.

It was enough. With a grunt of surprise the Confederate catapulted out of the saddle and hit the dirt. The sword fell a yard away. On hands and knees he started to crawl for it, scuttling as desperately as a beggar after a coin. Just as his fingers touched it, Macleod kicked it out of reach.

The men's eyes locked in hatred. Macleod looked towards where the sword lay. He took a step towards it, intending to use the blade to kill the man who had so mercilessly dispatched Hooker.

The bullet passing over his head brought him up short. In the horror of those last minutes he'd forgotten where he was. Now, another bullet kicking up dirt at his feet reminded him there was danger all around him as the enemy closed in.

Logic vied with rage and the thirst for revenge. For sure, the Confederates' bullets would kill him. He was as good as done for. No way out. The redhead's hand was grasping at his ankle and he kicked out at him viciously, forcing him to let go. His eyes alighted on the horse. The animal could give him a chance, a slim one, but he would have to give up the struggle with his enemy and take it now or he'd succumb to one of those bullets any minute. Resolved to try to live, he grasped the reins and leapt into the saddle.

As he kicked the animal's flanks, he glanced down at the redhead. His eyes were riveted on Macleod and he was trying to pull his gun from his holster. The Negro knew he would never forget that face as long as he lived, the fury and evil malice emanating from it. For a second he hesitated, wanting to kill the man and avenge Hooker, but he knew more delay would be costly so he kicked the horse into action, spurring it away from the enemy and out towards the bluff below which he knew lay the Mississippi River and his best escape route.

He was thankful he was a good rider. Bullets screeched over his head but he kept low in the saddle, his eyes on the bluff, investing his life in making the distance. With luck and good horsemanship, he reached it unscathed but, looking down, he realized it was a steeper declivity to the river than he'd expected. If the horse lost its footing it would mean the end. Yet, over his shoulder, he could see two horsemen not more than a hundred yards behind him. He heard their whoops, like hounds baying when they scent prey. As they sped towards him, their drawn swords coruscated in the sunlight. Figuring it was do or die, he urged the horse over the edge and let it have its head.

The animal's knees buckled once, nearly dislodging him, but it righted itself again and continued its descent while he clung on to its neck praying for deliverance. At last it reached the bottom and the river spread out ahead of him like a grey blanket. He urged the horse into the water as his pursuers fired down from the bluff.

The horse, game enough, started to swim but ten yards out Macleod felt it go limp under him, knew a bullet had found a fatal spot. There was nothing for it but to abandon the animal, start swimming himself. Fear of those men on the ridge above driving him on, he eased his feet out of the stirrups and slid under the water.

When he surfaced, a bullet kicked up spray a foot from his face so he went under again, propelled himself towards the far shore. Lungs at bursting point, he surfaced further out. Bullets ploughing into the surrounding water told him he was still target-practice and he plunged again. That repetitious, deadly game of cat and mouse seemed to go on for ever, driving him to the limits of his endurance, but his luck and his lungs held. Each time he came up, he expected a bullet to end it for him yet the Confederates' aim didn't improve. In the end, maybe because the evening had drawn in and the light was a little poorer, or maybe because there was more excitement back in the fort, they gave him up as a lost cause. Glancing back over his shoulder, he saw the bluff was completely deserted and he was able to swim the half-mile to the far shore unimpeded.

When he emerged from the Mississippi, he was still in shock. Visions of Hooker's head balancing grotesquely on his shoulders, its long spiralling tumble to the ground, the dead eyes staring soullessly up at him, gnawed their way back into his mind. He thought they would never let him rest until they had burrowed a place in his consciousness for ever.

Though he was exhausted, he knew it was best just to keep walking westwards, away from Fort Pillow, away from those butchers and what he had witnessed. Keep moving, try not to think was his mantra. It had all been in vain, the war, the hope of freedom, everything. The Negro was no more to those Southerners than an animal who could be cut down like corn, regardless of a white flag. The hatred was so deep in those Southerners. Freedom was just a word. For the Negro, the world would always be troublesome; no matter how the war went, men like those would still be around to make sure of that.

2

The Tonkawa scout came across the flat plain at a gallop, heading for the small column of mounted troopers who, when they saw him coming, reined in. Sergeant Rutledge, at the head of the troop, took a swig from his canteen. His men drank too, figuring they might as well take advantage to ease their thirsts, because chasing Comanches out here on the Staked Plains was hard, relentless work. You never knew when there'd be a chance to slake your dried throat.

Sitting behind the sergeant, Private Jim Macleod of the 10th cavalry, Fort Sill, Indian Territory, was figuring that, hard as this life was, he was content, living a better way than he had in the previous four years or so since he'd escaped the slaughter at Fort Pillow. In those years he'd wandered aimlessly, had joined up with some pretty dubious characters and, filled with a devilish anger, had done things he was ashamed of now.

Eventually, he'd realized he couldn't go on that way and had headed back to South Texas, to his old home, to see his mother. Everything had changed since the end of the war and he was informed that his mother and brother had left the plantation, gone westward. Nobody he had asked had known their exact destination. The Freedmen's Bureau who, post war, specialized in finding relatives of dispersed slave families, tried to find them for him. No result had been forthcoming until a week ago, when they'd written that a Negro woman, name of Jesse Macleod, was living in rough country ten miles from Sweetwater, west Texas. On his next furlough he was figuring to head down to Sweetwater.

His thoughts returned to the present when the Tonkawa scout dismounted and hurried towards the sergeant. Macleod leaned towards the trooper next to him.

'He's seen 'em,' he stated. 'That feller only gets excited when there's Comanches around. . . . Hates them like the rest of his people after the Comanches slaughtered the most of them.'

'Seeing 'em is one thing,' the trooper said, 'catching them is another. They ride like the wind and they know this land. We been tail-chasing a week now.'

Macleod glanced at the sergeant who was still in animated conversation with the scout.

'Look at those two, though. Something's on the boil for sure.'

'There's only ten of us,' the trooper said, flicking a hand at a troublesome fly. 'The sarg ain't going to attack. He'll be reporting back to the main column first if he's got sense.'

The conversation with the scout ended abruptly and Sergeant Rutledge swung his horse round to face the men. Macleod knew the look. His features were set grimly, as though he'd just made a decision he was determined to see through to the end.

'We're under orders to kill any Comanche we find off the reservation,' he yelled, 'and the scout has seen a camp. He'll take us there and we'll wipe 'em out. There's enough of us. It'll be a feather in the cap for us colours.'

'That simple,' Macleod mumbled. 'Didn't know a Comanche raiding-party would sit around waiting to be attacked.'

'Tell that to the sergeant,' the trooper behind him piped up, 'and he'll have your black hide. We just do what we told and he's the man who does the telling. Just hope those feathers he's talking about aren't at the end of a Comanche war arrow.'

There was no time for further debate because the order came to ride at full gallop. The Tonkawa rode ahead across the flat ground. Eventually, they hit a gully where they dismounted and led the horses, the sergeant laying it down that he didn't want to hear so much as a squeak of saddle leather. Before long, they emerged on to the flat again and led their animals up the narrow incline. Following the Tonkawa's example, they left their horses tethered just below the rise and flat-bellied it to the top.

Macleod found himself staring into a shallow decline. Below him were a collection of brush shelters, the kind the Indians used when they didn't intend to hang around too long. He could see no braves, only women and children skinning buffalo-hides, a few old men smoking together. There was a domestic peacefulness to the scene that he almost envied and one thing he knew for certain was that Lone Wolf, the Nokoni leader, and the younger men who had broken out with him were absent. Most likely they were away raiding. The camp below clearly contained those who followed him but could not fight, thus it would make no sense to attack. He wondered if the Tonkawa's hatred of the Comanche had led him to mislead the sergeant. Surely, now he could see the situation for himself, Rutledge wouldn't attack but report back that they'd found where Lone Wolf was holed up.

He was disabused of that notion when he heard Rutledge's order passing down the line.

'We're going in. Shoot to kill.'

Macleod's mouth dropped open. He caught the eye of the man next to him.

'They're just women, boys and old men. This can't be.'

'Sarg has orders to wipe out all the red fellers who broke out. Guess that means all. Just do it, Macleod. We get the job done we get back to the main column quicker.'

Macleod gripped his rifle hard until the knuckles showed white. He could hardly believe this was happening. Hadn't their own people suffered enough cruelties for them to know you didn't make war on the weak and helpless? He felt a sense of total despair. Flashbacks to the slaughter he'd witnessed at Fort Pillow returned to haunt him once again. Were his people no better than those Confederate cavalry? What was the difference? He felt sick to his stomach and his mind went numb.

17

When the command came and the troopers rose, the habit of obedience to orders made him stand up with them. As they began the descent into the camp, weapons at the ready, he automatically conformed, while in another part of his brain he tried to deny this could be happening. These men walking down the hill to do this thing were his kind. Some he counted as friends. Surely at the last minute someone or something would intervene.

The first one to see them coming was a woman. She opened her mouth to sound a warning but her cry was aborted by a soldier's bullet. Like startled deer, captured in that moment before flight, the Comanches looked up the rise and saw the blue uniforms. They started to run, the older men, who had been smoking contentedly a moment ago, trying to help the old women and children along the gully to the remuda where the horses, disturbed by the gunfire, pawed the ground restlessly.

Macleod saw a boy no more than twelve years old pick up a bow and arrow. Before he could fit the arrow, a bullet knocked him off his feet as though he was cardboard.

Every step he made was taken reluctantly, like a man wading upriver against an opposing current, but Macleod kept going while the troopers beside him fired down at the fleeing Indians. Another woman went down. He heard a trooper whoop. The Negro next to him in line shouted enthusiastically: 'It's a turkey-shoot.'

Macleod's legs no longer felt part of him. It was as though he was disembodied, watching it all from somewhere above, a place where he could deny he had any real part of it. When the soldiers entered the camp and started to walk through, he had not yet raised his own rifle to fire a shot. He was with them in body for sure, but his spirit was trying to escape.

His full faculties returned when a woman broke cover and brushed against him as she ran past. That physical human contact seemed to bring him back to life. He watched Sergeant Rutledge chase after the woman like a great, clumsy bear after a sleek elk. It looked as though she might make the remuda but her foot hit a boulder and she tumbled. Before she could rise the sergeant was standing over her and reloading his rifle. He lifted his weapon to his shoulder. His finger tightened on the trigger as he aimed down at the stricken woman who was calmly accepting that her time had come.

'Enough!' Macleod yelled. He came up behind Rutledge fast and struck him hard between the shoulder-blades with the butt of his rifle.

The sergeant staggered under the force of the blow. His rifle fired but the bullet missed the target and ricocheted harmlessly off a rock. When he swung around angrily, Macleod was standing over the woman, his rifle shouldered and pointed at Rutledge's heart.

The sergeant's look turned from anger to outraged amazement. At first, he'd thought a Comanche had come at him from behind. But this was one of his own men.

'What the hell you doing?'

'I'm taking the woman out of here,' Macleod

answered. 'There's enough blood on your hands this day.'

He was aware that the gunfire had died away now, giving way to an eerie silence pressing in on all sides. When he looked around, dead Comanches were scattered through the camp and the troopers, the business done, were starting to point in his direction, wondering what was happening between him and Rutledge. They started towards him from all sides.

'Drop the rifle, Rutledge!' Macleod ordered, 'and do it quick 'cos I'm mad enough right now to drop you like you dropped those people.'

One look into Macleod's eyes was enough for the sergeant to comply. He let the rifle fall.

'You gone crazy, Macleod?' he said. 'You're in a real bad mess, holding a weapon on a superior.'

The troopers were circling him now. They'd heard the sergeant's last words and he was aware of their eyes upon him, waiting for his next move. He looked down at the woman who was motionless and staring up at him. He could see that whatever she was, she wasn't pure-bred Comanche. He hazarded a guess:

'You're Mexican, yes?'

She nodded her head in reply.

'Not even Comanche.' He spat the words at the men surrounding him. 'But what difference does that make when you got that bloodlust.'

He leaned over, offered the woman his hand. She reached up to take it and he pulled her to her feet. The men took a step closer to him, their rifles, waist high, pointing in his direction.

'Cut him down!' Rutledge ordered.

'You'll be the first to die!' Macleod told him. 'Me and the woman are going out of here and you're going to walk us to the remuda. Go on, git ahead!'

Something in Macleod's demeanour convinced the sergeant that it was no idle threat. Shaking his head, he started for the remuda. Macleod followed him, leading the woman, his eyes circling the troopers, his expression one of disgust, as though he could smell the odour from all the dung-hills in Texas right here under his nose. Strangely, one or two troopers dropped their heads.

'Like some of you I fought in a war for freedom and saw terrible things,' he shouted, giving vent to all his frustration. 'But what good was it when the slave was no better than his master. All you brave men proved that today, following Rutledge like sheep.'

None of them spoke. They just kept clear and let him go. He was half-expecting one of them to chance his luck, but they just stood there motionless.

A voice called after him. 'You're damn right, Macleod! This was a bad day's work.'

Still holding the rifle on Rutledge, he cut out the best two mustangs. He helped the woman on to one, climbed on to the other himself. For a moment, as he settled on the horses' back, his rifle wavered. The sergeant had been waiting for a chance and made a grab for it but Macleod saw him coming. In one smooth action, he reversed the weapon and with a swift jabbing motion let him have the rifle butt right on his jawbone. Rutledge staggered backwards, then went down, insensible.

Twenty yards away the soldiers watched it happen.

Before they had a chance to react, Macleod struck the woman's horse on the flank and dug his heels in. He kept behind the woman and low on the mustang's neck but no shots followed them as they sped away.

When they'd run for half a mile, he grabbed the woman's reins and slowed both horses to a standstill. He could see no sign of pursuit but, off to the left of the camp, a dust cloud was heading fast towards the soldiers. The woman saw it too and, in a fearful gesture, covered her mouth with her hand.,

'Lone Wolf,' she said, a quiver in her voice.

'The troopers ain't seen him. Too distracted, the damn fools.'

The woman's lip began to tremble. Just above a whisper, she said: 'They are dead men.'

For a moment, because of old loyalties, he was tempted to ride back to help. Common sense told him that would be a useless gesture and, anyway, did his erstwhile companions deserve it? Fate could decide whether they lived or died. He couldn't make a difference even if he wanted to.

He turned to the woman. 'You can go back if you want.'

Soon as he said it, her eyes widened and, as though from the depths of her being, her fear sprang at him.

'Never!' she stated. 'I could endure it no more. I think God sent you to help me. Please take me away.'

He shook his head. 'Don't think God was anything to do with it,' he said. 'But there ain't time to debate it. Let's both take ourselves as far away as we can before sunset.'

*

Lone Wolf sat astride his pinto and watched his men torturing those bluecoats who had been unfortunate enough to survive the attack. They were drawing the process out, fuelled by their anger at the slaughter of their loved ones. When they were finished, they would bury their families and there would be much grief. He wondered how much respect it would all cost him. Would his people still believe in his *puha*, his power?

He walked the pinto towards the remuda, ran his expert eyes over the horses and realized in an instant that the best two were missing. Soon, he had found fresh tracks; two riders heading away southwards. When he saw the imprints of army-issue boots and, next to them, bare-feet marks, he knew a soldier and a girl had ridden away not long ago.

He walked the pinto through the remuda, heard a groan.. When he looked down a soldier was lying there in the dust. In an instant, he removed his lasso from the pommel and threw it round the shoulders of the bluecoat who was trying to prop himself up on one elbow. Kicking his heels into the horse, he dragged the man clear of the remuda.

Rutledge, who had hardly had time or the sensibility fully to realize what had happened to him, looked up through blurred vision to see a buffalo-scalp with protruding horns hovering over him. His eyes travelled downwards. Under the headdress a face painted with two black stripes across the forehead was peering into his own. He wondered if he was dreaming it but his faculties were reviving steadily and when a knife glinted in Indian's hand, it brought him to his full senses and he remembered everything.

Lone Wolf dragged Rutledge to his feet, spun him round so he could survey the whole camp. His vision was sharp enough to take in what the Comanches were doing. On Lone Wolf's command two braves tied rawhide ropes to a soldier's arms and legs. Then they walked their horses in different directions, stretching the trooper's body until it was as taut as a bowstring just before the arrow's release. Rutledge shut his eyes tight but his ears couldn't shut out the man's unearthly screams as his arms and legs popped out of the sockets.

Lone Wolf pushed him to his knees, squatted in front of him and held the knife in front of his eyes.

'If you tell me the name of the soldier who rode out of the camp, I will only slit your throat.' He gestured towards the soldier's racked body, 'or you will die like that, squealing like a pig.'

Through narrowed eyes, Rutledge glanced at the blade's honed edge. He felt regret that the end of his life had come so quickly, so surprisingly, up on him. There was so much he wished to do and, he could see now, so much to regret. His frustration raged like a fire inside him. With nowhere to escape, it condensed to a sharper flame, a white-hot resentment of the man who he considered had rendered him helpless in the hour of danger. The Comanche beast would have Macleod's name all right and, he hoped, the traitor's life.

'Macleod,' he rasped. 'He rode off with a Mexican woman. I hope you kill the bastard.'

Lone Wolf straightened. So the Mexican woman had survived, gone with the soldier. He grunted, put the knife to Rutledge's throat and, with a powerful, sideways motion of his arm, ended the sergeant's life.

The chief remounted his horse, remembering now that he already knew one Macleod, but he was white, not a buffalo soldier like the men who had slaughtered his people here. For sure, it was a name he would not forget. He had business south of here. He would try to find the soldier's trail and kill him, so that all the whites in Texas would know that the soldiers had paid to the last man for what they had done. The return of the Mexican woman would be good. She was his second favourite wife.

3

Macleod wished there was more cover, that this part of Texas wasn't so flat. If the landscape had been different he would have holed up at nightfall, given the horses and the woman somewhere to rest in reasonable security. But he wasn't confident about their safety so, apart from one brief respite to water the mustangs, he kept them on the move most of the night. Better to be safe than sorry in easy tracking country.

A couple of hours before daylight they rode into a shallow creek-bed. He decided they couldn't go on much longer and called a halt. While the horses ate grass and drank from the stream, he and the woman settled beside the bank. During the long ride they had hardly spoken, each preoccupied with the magnitude of what had happened back there, its implications for their futures. Now they were too tired from the hard ride for conversation and, in spite of the cold, fell straight asleep.

Macleod woke first at the crack of dawn, felt inside his tunic and extracted the letter he'd received from the Freedman's Bureau. He was reading it when the woman's eyes opened. He noticed how exhausted she looked. Yet, on that long ride, she had never complained. He saw, too, that under the grime and dust she was a fine-looking woman, dark -haired and strong-featured, with a certain dignity about her that life amongst the Comanche had not touched.

'You got family?' he asked. 'People looking for you?'

She shook her head, pushed her long hair over her shoulders.

'No, nobody.'

Macleod knew from the melancholy tone of voice what had happened.

'You have a home?'

She turned her dark eyes in his direction. He saw the hurt and sadness there.

'The Comanche burned my home and killed my family.'

After a moment's silence, he said, 'How long have you been with the Comanche?'

Her eyes dropped. 'One year, I think.'

He knew the Comanche, knew just how hard it was for a woman. The squaws worked hard from sunrise to sunset, aged prematurely.

'What's your name, ma'am?'

'Maria.'

He shook his head. 'Well, Maria, you did well to survive. Some captives don't. You must have some guts.'

'Perhaps,' she said, in a scarcely audible voice.

Macleod waved the letter at her. 'I think I got family two days' ride from here. Probably best you

27

and I head there. You're just about done in. Maybe we can stay there awhile.'

She frowned at him. 'You – think – you have family?'

'It's a long story, a complicated one.'

'Tell me.'

He hesitated, drew a deep breath.

'I left my family to fight in the war. Afterwards I went back but things had changed. My brother and my mother had left. This letter reckons my mother could be near Sweetwater, has a map of the location. Chances are my brother is with her.'

'Then you must find this place. If they are there, they will be joyed to see you. Yes?'

Macleod smiled sardonically. 'My mother, yes. My brother . . .' He left it hanging.

'What of your brother? You do not like him?'

He sighed, not comfortable with the subject.

'Ever see a white negro?'

She shook her head, puzzled.

'There is no such thing!'

He laughed. 'Well, anyway, my brother is white. We have the same father but I was the burnt cake and he was the icing.'

She nodded her head as though she understood, but said nothing.

'I think we're safe,' he said, changing the subject. He rose, reached down and helped her up.

'I have not thanked you, yet,' she said as she dusted herself down. 'Forgive me. I know what it has cost you to save me.'

'Maybe you saved me, Maria. We don't know the

outcome when that dust cloud hit the troopers.'

Later, when they had mounted the mustangs and were heading south, he was surprised at himself, how easy it had been to open up to the woman about his family. But there were things he hadn't told her. How his father had owned the plantation. How his coloured mother had been his father's mistress and had borne him two sons, Aaron and himself. How Aaron, with his white skin, had orientated towards the big house, been indulged by their father, even after their father had married a white woman and had family with her.

For himself, he stayed with his mother in the slave quarters, worked in the fields, resisting any attempts by his father to give him advantages. Aaron flitted between the slave quarters and the big house, like a man with a split personality, never completely at home in either place. His mother, rejected by the master after his marriage, never complained, never saw Aaron's behaviour as disloyalty to her. In some ways Macleod understood and forgave Aaron much because his brother did love their mother. But his mother had just been used like the slave she was; that stuck in his craw and he figured it hadn't bothered his brother enough.

'I was one of Lone Wolf's wives.' The woman's voice broke into his thoughts bringing him back to the present.

Her mentioning it now came as a surprise but he knew she hadn't needed to say anything. She was trusting him with it.

He turned to look at her. 'Does that mean he'll be

coming after you? Is that why you're telling me?'

She shrugged. 'I don't think so. He has too much to do and he has other wives.'

He saw the worried look cross her face, considered that, in spite of her words, she was concerned. After what she'd been through, how could it be otherwise.

'He knows the army are after him. He'll be too busy hiding to give you a thought.'

'I hope so,' she said. 'I could not stand to return to him.'

'I'll see to it you don't,' he told her, then wondered why he'd said that instantly, why she had obviously aroused a protective instinct in him. Didn't he have enough troubles himself without making her promises?

Over the next two days, through instinct and knowledge gleaned from patrols he'd ridden, Macleod took them across the Staked Plains and southwards, further into Texas. Eventually, he was able to recognize landmarks indicated on the map the bureau had sent him. From then on it was easy and, early on the morning of the third day, he could see dwellings on the spot where he hoped to find his mother.

'Guess it ain't much, Maria,' he remarked as they came within 200 yards of the buildings. 'A cabin and a barn is all.'

She shot him a reproving glance. 'It depends what you were expecting.'

Fifty yards out, he said: 'Looks deserted! Hope we haven't—'

His sentence remained unfinished, drowned by

the shot that rang out from the cabin. The bullet lifted dirt ten yards in front of them, causing the horses to shy nervously.

'State your business!'

Macleod thought the voce that followed the bullet was familiar. He screwed up his eyes and peered at the cabin but all he could see were boarded-up windows. The door was slightly ajar and he guessed that that was where the shot had come from and would be where the owner of the voice was watching from. He wanted to shout out his mother's name but inexplicably her name caught in his throat and he couldn't get it out.

'Water,' he yelled eventually, playing for time. 'We just want to water the horses, then we'll be gone.'

There was a long silence. Then the same voice rang out again.

'Trough's near the barn. Come ahead.'

As they urged the mustangs forward, he was aware of the woman's scrutinizing him. He knew she was wondering why he was being evasive.

'Couldn't come right out with it,' he muttered. 'It's been so long.'

He couldn't tell her he was nervous now. It seemed an age since he'd run away from the plantation to join the Northern army. He was no longer a youth but a man who'd seen and done hellish things. He'd done them for the most part in the name of freedom but, in those wandering years after Fort Pillow, he'd gone purely bad for a while. Then he'd busted some broncs for the army and they'd encouraged him to enlist. Joining up had saved him, that was, until recent events had turned against him. He hoped his mother, if she was indeed inside, would understand when he told her his story. He doubted his brother would.

Aware they were still watched, they watered the horses. Once the animals had drunk their fill, Macleod started to walk his horse towards the building. Maria following him.

When they were ten yards off a tall man stepped out and pointed a rifle at them. Macleod recognized him instantly. He was bigger and more muscular, probably the result of manual labour in this hard land, but it was his brother, no mistake, though the only resemblance between them a stranger might have noted was the tight, thickly curled hair and broad shoulders.

'We don't welcome deserters here,' his brother rasped. 'And you're a deserter, mister. For sure, nobody rides out here alone in uniform with a woman dressed like a Comanche squaw lessen he's a deserter. Just be on your way.'

Macleod had kept his head low and his hat pulled down. Now, he slowly pushed back his hat and lifted his head. He looked straight at his brother.

'A man is more than the sum of his parts, Aaron. People assume too much, 'specially white folks. You know that, don't you, brother.'

Macleod saw perplexity and confusion spreading over his brother's features. A ghost had just walked back into his life, transformed into flesh and blood before his eyes in an instant. He was struggling to accept what his eyes were telling him.

'You going to invite your brother and this lady into your house like a good old Southern boy, Aaron? Or are you going to keep us waiting out here?'

Aaron lowered the rifle and came towards him, his hand outstretched. Macleod grasped it tight and they shook hands.

'We were told you were dead,' Aaron muttered. 'Killed at Fort Pillow.'

'That wasn't far wrong,' he answered enigmatically, before gesturing at the woman. 'This here's Maria. She's had a bad time with the Comanche: Lone Wolf and his Nokonis. I'll tell you about that later. Right now, I'd like to see my mother. The Freedman's Bureau put me on to this place, said a Negro woman name of Macleod was here. Where is she? Inside?'

He took a step towards the hut. Aaron put a hand on his shoulder to restrain him. Their eyes met and Aaron's dropped away first.

'You're a week too late,' he said. 'She died with your name on her lips. Thought she was going to heaven to meet you. Religious to the end, I guess.'

Macleod could feel the tears forming. His mother who had sacrificed so much for him, who had been so strong, was gone, before he had even a chance to explain why he'd run away. He'd always consoled himself with the thought that she'd have understood his reasons, but he'd have liked the chance to make his peace with her, return some of the care she'd given him. It hit him harder than a mule's kick that the opportunity had gone, that he would never see her again.

Aaron's hand remained on his shoulder.

'I buried her behind the hut,' he said. 'There's a small cross. The preacher came out and said some words. Go and take a look. I'll fix some grub.'

As he walked to the back, Macleod felt as though he'd been battered body and soul. After all these years to miss his mother by a week seemed the work of a perverse fate. He found the cross and knelt down, spoke the things he'd meant to say to his mother's face. He stayed there a long time before he rose, took a few minutes to control his emotions, then headed inside.

Maria's eyes followed him as he took a seat at the table. He studied the room, thinking it held no more than the bare necessities, was not much better than the slave quarters. Yet, it was clean and neat and he recognized his mother's touch everywhere, like familiar imprints in sand after the traveller has departed.

Aaron, sensing his deep melancholy, was silent, just passed him the bread and meat and pushed the coffee-pot towards him. For a long while, nobody spoke, then Maria broke the silence.

'I have told Aaron what happened to us, that you had to desert to save my life.'

Aaron eyed him. 'It's a big country. You'll have to lose yourself.'

Macleod couldn't help his reaction. He wanted to hit out at something or someone, release the tension of old hurts which were resurfacing now with the sudden news of his mother's death. He glared at Aaron.

'Don't worry! I don't intend hanging round here to cause you embarrassment. Doesn't do to have a colour for a brother, does it? Cramp your style, uh! I always reminded you of what you truly were, didn't I?'

Aaron's lip curled. 'Who was it ran off and who was it stayed to look after our mother and then brought her here after the war?'

Macleod let his eyes roam round the room with an air of disdain.

'This place ain't much better than the slave quarters. The plantation was sold off, wasn't it, Aaron, and our dear father when he died, left you nothing. His other boys got what little was left. I know! I went back! He took you for a fool Aaron, a convenient plaything, just like he did our mother. That white skin he gave you don't change nothing. End of the day, he knew if you had a child, chances were it would be black.'

Aaron's fist came down hard on the table.

'Damn you! He was our father. He left me a pure-bred horse to breed on. That's what I'm doing here.'

Macleod laughed. 'Pure-bred, eh! He still had a sense of humour then. What colour?'

Aaron sighed, controlled his temper.

'You ain't changed. You ran off and left our mother and I picked up the pieces. Now you try to twist it round to ease your conscience. Mother never did understand why you had to fight against your own people.'

'My own people!' Macleod shook his head. 'Meaning our father or the South? Neither meant a diddly to me long as I was a slave. Our father shamed

35

our mother like she was nothing and you kissed his backside. Mother was taught to think it was the order of things. Bred into her, wasn't it? But I left to fight for my kind, our kind. Different with you though, brother. You thought that skin of yours made you better than the field hands and your father indulged you. Must have pained you to have to trail our mother here. Was she an embarrassment?'

Maria had been looking from one to the other as the argument raged. The bitterness between them was almost tangible, the atmosphere tense. She tried to intervene and pacify them.

'This should not be,' she pleaded. 'Think of your mother. She would not like this argument between her sons.'

Her words hit a nerve with Macleod. Now that he had let out all that steam, he started to regret it. It was old ground best left undisturbed and, in truth, he understood it must have been difficult for his brother to live in that white skin. He guessed it would have been better for Aaron to have left the plantation years ago. Their father should have granted him his freedom and advised that.

'Truth is, you and me ain't like brothers, no matter how mother tried to make it be,' he said, in a more conciliatory tone. 'You chose to distance yourself. All I need from you now is a change of clothes and accommodation for Maria till she gets her strength back. Tomorrow, I'll head out for Sweetwater. I got cash wired to the bank when I knew I was going to head this way on my next furlough. When I come back, we'll leave.'

'Do what you want,' Aaron told him. 'You always do anyway. You and Maria can sleep in the barn. You'll find blankets in there. It's warm and comfortable enough.'

They finished the meal in silence. Macleod stood up and headed for the door, Maria following. He turned on the threshold.

'Least you took care of Mother,' he grunted. 'Was she happy here, Aaron?'

'Happy as she could be. Missed all her old friends but most of 'em had scattered anyway. There was just her and me out here but we went into Sweetwater all the time and she liked that.'

Macleod nodded. 'Good! I'm glad you did right by her. It would mean everything to her.' He added ungrudgingly 'I'm grateful to you for that.'

Before they stepped outside, Maria spoke up. 'Do the Comanches never come here?'

'They come, once in a while,' Aaron told her, 'But I've always traded with them so they've left me alone. I keep a store of things they like, so I guess they figure it would be bad business to harm me. Can't say they don't make me nervous though. I got some horses they likely fancy.'

Maria looked unnerved as she slipped through the door behind Macleod.

'Don't worry,' he told her, seeing her concern, 'I'm sure I hid our trail pretty good. Lessen he knew where we were headed, it would take him too long to follow us. He'll have better things to do with the army out looking.'

Maria stared out across the prairie as they headed

for the barn. A wild dog yelped plaintively some-where in the darkness, like a soul lost in the universe, frightened by the incalculable possibilities lurking in its infinite vastness. She shuddered and hoped Aaron was right about the Comanches.

There were five horses stabled in the barn. One was a magnificent black, pure-bred. Macleod admired it as they climbed the ladder to the upper tier where they would sleep. He figured it must be the horse their father had bequeathed to Aaron.

'Sorry I lost it back there,' he said, as they settled into their blankets. 'Old wounds not healed is all. Not polite opening them up in front of you.'

She looked at him shrewdly. 'He seems OK, your brother.'

'He'll be OK with us, just as long as he hasn't to admit to no white folks that I'm related. He knows folk will never look at him the same after they know.'

She hesitated, then said: 'You know, sometimes a gringo looks at a Mexican or a Comanche as though they were God's leftovers. Believe me, I know the look. Your brother was not like that with either of us.'

Macleod turned over, pulled the blanket over his shoulders.

'Then maybe there's hope for him yet,' he opined. 'But I've seen the look when he's been around white folk with me there.'

Before he drifted off to sleep, he thought about the woman. She was the reason he'd deserted but he guessed she was worth it. She had an uncomplaining spirit, that one, yet there was a sensitivity there too which reminded him of his mother. Memories began creeping back but for now he shut them out. There would be plenty of time for them when he had the woman in a safe town and himself where the army would forget him.

4

Bright and early next morning, Macleod borrowed a saddle and rode out for Sweetwater in civilian clothes that his brother lent him. Before he departed he had seen Maria's trepidation, had felt compelled to reassure her he wasn't going to be gone more than a day and, when he returned, they'd keep riding until they were somewhere Lone Wolf would never reach her. His brother told her that she had nothing to be concerned about but, as he had ridden away, Macleod had seen the worry-lines etched deeply on her features and knew neither of them had succeeded in allaying her fear of Comanches. He guessed that would take a long time to leave her system. For some captives, when they were freed, their experiences stayed with them and drove them mad.

Sweetwater wasn't a big town but it did possess a bank. He withdrew his transferred savings after the due processes were completed, then strolled over to the general store, intending to buy himself a new hat and Maria some new clothes. He thought maybe getting out of those Comanche clothes and into new apparel would help her shed part of her arduous past, encourage her to look forward to a better life.

The store had only few customers so, after he had selected a hat for himself, in a low, embarrassed voice he asked the storekeep if they kept women's dresses. The patron, an old-timer with a pleasant manner, scrutinized him, his eyes betraying his amazement at the big man's sheepishness. Macleod was grateful his black skin hid his blushes as he was shown to another room in the depths of the store.

'Hope we got your size,' the man said, laughing as he left him to choose from a rack of dresses. 'Take your time now, big feller, and try 'em on if you're so inclined. We're always looking for new custom, 'specially in the outsizes.'

It was delivered with good humour and Macleod laughed with him. Long exposure to it as a slave had given him an ear that knew when humour was mean and spiteful. This man was just joshing him, no malice there at all and it was good to laugh after the tension of the last days.

While he was choosing a dress which approximated to Maria's size, he heard voices coming from the main part of the store; it seemed that business had woken up for the old man. Those voices grew louder. One of them rose above the others, thrusting itself painfully into Macleod's memory with its overweening, Southern intonations. For a moment, he froze on the spot. Then he shook his head, chasing away the horrors the voice had sent galloping through his brain in a stampede of images he wanted to banish for ever, yet at the same time, paradoxically, wished never to forget. Voices, like looks, could be similar, couldn't they? His mind was surely playing tricks. Maybe his nervous system was all strung up, full of imaginings.

Calming himself, he selected the dress, started for the main room. In the doorway he halted, rooted to the spot. That voice again! Now he could see the mean mouth it issued from, that face he could never forget, the one that still haunted his nightmares.

Yet, even with the evidence before him, there was a moment when he disbelieved his own eyes, thought it impossible their trails would cross here. But everything about the man was burned deep inside him, like a brand that always smoulders. That red hair, that freckled face belonged unmistakably to the Confederate who had executed his friend Hooker. Chance, fate, justice, whatever, had brought his enemy to this small town and he was ripe for killing. All his being wanted to march right up to him and kill him there and then.

Rationality had to prevail; he hadn't a prayer. His Colt was in his saddle pack and there were five men all wearing guns standing alongside the redhead. Best to walk straight out of the store, wait for a chance to face him alone. Then, he would avenge Hooker and all his comrades murdered under a white flag that day at Fort Pillow. By God, he would!

He pulled his hat low over his forehead and, the dress over his arm, headed towards the door. Red hair and his companions were a good ten feet away so he thought he would make it without them taking much notice.

'You gonna pay for the dress?'

The storekeep's enquiry brought him up short near the counter. Out of the corner of his eye, he noticed the men's heads swinging his way, was aware of their curiosity and cursed himself for his mistake.

He felt inside his jacket pocket, withdrew a bundle of notes, took a step up to the counter and faced the old man.

'Sorry about that,' he said, his voice low and husky. 'Just wanted to buy the dress and git out of here quick.'

The old man smiled, mistaking the cause of his discomfiture to be the dress as he took his money and gave him the change. He gestured at the dress.

'Wrap that for you if you like.'

'It's OK,' Macleod said, turning towards the door and sliding a sideways glance at the men who had gone quiet now and were still watching him.

He made three steps before that voice, the same sneer to it as that day at Fort Pillow, was hurled at him.

'Since when don't you remove your hat in the presence of white men, boy. You one of those who thinks the war changed things, that it?'

He turned to face the redhead, conscious that all the men's eyes were on him, waiting to see how he would react. Half-smiles played on their lips as they anticipated the prospect of a bit of fun at the Negro's expense. An air of assumed superiority oozed out of them. Though none of it was a new experience for Macleod, he still itched to wipe that arrogant complacency from their faces.

He ignored the impulse, controlled himself,

removed his hat, bowed his head and turned towards the door again. Behind him, he heard them sniggering. When he was a foot from the door, redhead's voice boomed again.

'Boy!'

Gritting his teeth, he turned. From behind his counter, the old man met his gaze. There was pity in his eyes.

'That colour of dress don't suit you, boy,' the redhead barked. 'Wrong for your skin shade, I'd say. Next time, ask for yeller.'

'Or maybe black with a yeller stripe,' one of the men added, to the general amusement.

Macleod's eyes burned across the distance between them. The redhead frowned and he looked puzzled.

'Do I know you, boy? There's something about you familiar.'

Macleod shook his head. 'No ba'as!' he said, controlling himself again, speaking with all the mock servility he could muster.

Reassured by this affectation of humility, the redhead relaxed.

'Git out of here,' he said, 'and think yourself lucky. I've hung your kind when they ain't removed their hats.'

This time he made his exit without interference. He wasted no time, hurrying up the street towards his horse which was still tethered outside the bank. His Colt was wrapped in a blanket strapped to the saddle. He slid it out, stuck it in his trouser belt and started back.

He had no plan. All he knew was that he had to kill that redhead here and now because he might never get another chance and he'd be failing Hoover and so many others if he let the opportunity pass.

When he was half-way up the street, he saw his man and two others emerge from the store and head for the hitching rail. They were too busy engaged in conversation to notice him heading their way until he was almost up on them. One of them nudged the redhead, pointed at Macleod who halted in the street and faced the boardwalk where they were standing.

They stared at him open-mouthed as they registered the Colt jutting from his belt, the wide-legged stance he had assumed and his steady gaze as he found them. It was a complete transformation from the docile Negro they had abased a few minutes back and an affront to their sense of the order of things.

Redhead recovered his composure and stepped to the edge of the boardwalk. The other two moved either side of him.

Macleod spoke first.

'Couldn't find a yeller dress,' he said. ' Tried to find a white flag of surrender but guess it wouldn't have done me much good, would it? Didn't help my friends at Fort Pillow.'

He watched realization slither slyly across redhead's face. For certain, he was remembering that shameful day which was what Macleod wanted him to do.

'Guess those Confederates who ignored the flag at Fort Pillow should be the ones wearing yeller dresses, uh!' he continued.

The redhead's smile spread slowly, stretched his thin lips.

'So that's where I saw you before. Now you're asking me to finish the job.'

'If you can kill a man who's armed and ready.'

An expectant silence permeated the air between them, swelled to bursting point. Macleod focused on the three men. He would try for his main target, the redhead, first. The other two, if they pulled on him, would be secondary and, if he survived, he'd take off before the two inside the building had a chance to enter the fray.

'Finish him, boys!' the redhead shouted and made his play.

Macleod saw the gun hand descend to the holster. Instantly he dived to his right, his fingers curling around his Colt, pulling it from his waistband. While he was still in the air, he heard the bullet whistle past his head. He hit the dirt hard, rolled and brought his gun up to squeeze a shot at the redhead. His adversary clutched his shoulder and yelled out but Macleod knew it was a flesh, not a killing wound.

The other men reacted, stepping between Macleod and the wounded redhead, shielding him as they reached for their guns. Neither managed to clear the holster, frustrated mid-motion by the rapid succession of rifle fire which kicked up dirt on the ground between them and their intended victim. One of the shots kicked up dust just in front of Macleod's face, letting him know he was included.

'Enough! Drop 'em!' The command rang out somewhere behind the Negro. He turned his head, saw a tall man in a large Stetson walking across the street, holding a rifle, looking as though he would use it if he had to.

Attracted by the gunfire, the two men who had remained in the store emerged with guns in their hands. Rifle bullets fired in rapid succession and placed accurately between their feet made them think twice. When they saw the tall man advancing, the rifle butt tucked against shoulder and cheek, they let their Colts slide to the boardwalk.

The man with the rifle was up close now.

'Tell the redheaded feller to stand where I can see him,' he stated.

The redhead stepped back into view. Macleod had dropped his gun but was sorely tempted to scoop it up again and finish what he'd set out to do. But the man in the Stetson seemed to sense what he was thinking.

'Don't try it!' he snapped in Macleod's direction.

'What you interfering for,' the redhead snapped, holding his shoulder. 'This Negro wanted a fight and he was getting one. Who the hell do you think you are?'

The rifleman pulled back the flap of his jacket to reveal a star.

'I'm a Texas Ranger and a town ain't the place for gun-play. Besides, I don't like an unfair fight.' He paused. 'Are you fellers going to leave peaceable or do I have to lock you up?'

Using his good arm, the redhead stooped to pick up his gun, holstered it and stepped off the board-walk. He glared at the tall Ranger and untethered his horse. The other men followed his lead and, when they were all mounted up, he shouted at Macleod.

'There'll be another time. I know it.'

Macleod rose to his feet. 'Count on it! Today you were lucky. Maybe next time I'll take off your head with a sword.'

'Move out!' the Ranger ordered. 'Never seen you boys in this town before and don't want to again.' He pointed at Macleod. 'Same goes for him.'

In brooding silence, the men swung their horses away and rode off down the street. The Ranger then turned his attention to Macleod. Under the brim of the Stetson, the Negro could see cool blue eyes studying him speculatively.

'He deserved to die,' Macleod said bitterly, 'and he will.'

'I'd bet on it,' the man agreed.

The words surprised Macleod who stared at the Ranger with renewed interest.

'The odds were against you today, feller. Besides that, I need William Gaunt or Red Bill, as some call him, alive. If you let me buy you a drink I'll explain just why. Maybe you'll even want to help me.'

Half an hour later, Macleod found himself in the saloon pouring out the story of what had happened at Fort Pillow. The man listened without interrupting.

'So you see,' Macleod finished, 'I have good reason to want him dead.'

The Ranger wiped beer-froth from his moustache and shook his head.

'Now I know what you meant by that last remark,'

'bout taking his head off with a sword. Truth is none of what you told me is a surprise. Red Bill is known in Texas for killing Negroes. The war changed nothing for him. He thinks they're still slaves and should act that way.'

Macleod gave him a puzzled glance. 'Then why did you let him go today.'

'He's been breaking the law in all kinds of ways but he's never been pinned down. Witnesses have been too scared or he's done his dirty work in secret. We know, but we can't prove anything. Not yet.'

'But you will?'

'You bet. We've got ways of knowing his movements now and we think he's fixed a rendezvous with the Comanches, Lone Wolf's bunch. Bartering horses stolen by the Injuns and selling them down in Mexico is a lucrative business, 'specially if you throw in a few slaves provided by the Indians.'

For a moment, Macleod was tempted to tell him about his own recent experience with the Indians but he checked himself. Telling people you were a deserter wasn't a wise move, no matter that this man seemed a sympathetic listener.

'I heard the Nokoni led by Lone Wolf are on the prowl,' Macleod stated.

'News must travel fast,' the Ranger said. 'We've just heard a cavalry patrol was wiped out by that bunch. There were no survivors. The scouts found 'em tortured to death. Apparently they'd attacked a Comanche camp and were caught in the act.'

Macleod grimaced. Dying at the hands of Comanche torturers was the worst way to go and some of those men, in spite of what had happened that day, had been his friends. Then he realized that as far as the army was concerned, he was dead too, killed by the Comanches with the others. It meant they wouldn't be coming after him and, God willing, he could start a new life without constantly looking over his shoulder.

'These Comanches Red Bill is meeting. You sure it's the same lot?'

'Sure enough,' the Ranger told him. 'I'm telling you in confidence 'cos I was going to suggest you join us. Saw back there you got guts and we need men like you. We're going after Red Bill with nine men and he has twenty. It would be one way you could kill him legal.'

Macleod didn't know how to answer. For sure, he owed it to his comrades who died at Fort Pillow to avenge them. But Maria was his responsibility right now and he'd promised to take her somewhere safe. Yet, if it was Lone Wolf's band trading with Red Bill, maybe two problems could be solved in one go.

'Got responsibilities,' he said, eventually. 'Got folk on a ranch near here I'd have to talk to first.'

The Ranger drained his beer.

'It'll be a few days before we head out. See what you can do.'

5

Lone Wolf dismounted, squatted and studied the tracks. Two riders had stopped on this spot. One of them, judging by the marks his boots had made, was a soldier, the other a barefooted woman. His lips drew back, showing his teeth in a self-satisfied, lupine smile. Thanks to the sergeant, he knew the soldier's name. The girl with him must be the Mexican woman he had made one of his wives. He had cut their trail on several occasions, in spite of the attempts made to hide it.

Another time he might have ignored the tracks because he had a rendezvous to make. Time and the possibility that soldiers would be trailing him would not allow a deviation from his route. Now he stood and gazed across the plain in the direction the two fugitives had ridden. From hunting buffalo in better days a picture of this land was imprinted in his brain, so he allowed his thoughts to travel along the way they had chosen. He gave a snort of self-satisfaction when, in his mind's eye, their trail traversed the land he knew as Macleod's.

The name was the same as the buffalo soldier's. He

supposed that could be coincidence but preferred to think it was the work of his guiding spirit. All the soldiers who slaughtered his people had to die. It would go a little way to restoring his warriors' belief in his power if he brought vengeance to the only soldier to escape it and, in the process, recaptured his wife. At Macleod's place, he remembered seeing a horse he had coveted, a magnificent horse for breeding. It was another reason to go there. The gods were leading him, surely.

As he remounted, Long Nose rode up beside him. He followed his chief's gaze across the plain.

'What do you see, Lone Wolf?' he asked.

The chief swivelled his eyes towards him and made his decision, thinking the omens were fair and it was too good an opportunity to miss.

'The gods have shown me a place,' he said. 'We will find a pony soldier there with the Mexican woman. There is also a fine horse which we will take.'

'How far?'

'Two hours ride. Pick five braves, Long Nose. Let the others continue with our herd. We will catch up before the sun falls.'

Long Nose turned his horse, rode back to the main party to do his chief's bidding. When the five were selected they rode out behind their chief at full gallop. As the miles sped by they recognized the country, knew their direction would take them towards the place known as Macleod's where, in the past, they had traded. Because of his usefulness, they'd left him alone. Judging by Lone Wolf's promises, that usefulness would no longer keep him alive.

*

Aaron Macleod leaned on the fence watching the stallion prance around the perimeter of the corral. True, as his brother had so willingly pointed out, their father hadn't left him any property or money at the end, but this horse, the old man's final gift, was a fine specimen. He'd bred from him and made a tidy profit, which he intended to invest in buying more animals of good stock. His future, his chance of making something of himself depended entirely on that magnificent animal.

He was worried that his brother had come here. Nobody in the area knew his origins and he'd passed himself off as a white man, his mother as his old nanny, because it was safer that way. In spite of the new freedom Negroes were still given a hard time. Aaron knew of brotherhoods forming in parts of Texas to keep them in their place, to prevent them rising above their station. If he prospered and they found out about him he feared that one night he'd wake up to find the place surrounded by nightriders come to burn him out. His brother could be a problem if he stayed around too long and used the same name. Someone might get curious about the past and start investigating.

He heard the Mexican woman approach, watched her lean against the corral. He could see the strain of what she had endured in her face, felt sorry for her. Yet, the quicker she was gone the better. If the Comanches found out about her there would be hell to play.

53

'It is a pity you and your brother dislike each other so much,' she said.

He glanced in her direction. 'We don't dislike each other. We're just different, is all. He expected me to act the slave. Me, I thought to use my assets.'

Her eyes narrowed disapprovingly. 'You mean your white skin?'

'Got it in one.'

'I think he believes you rejected him.'

He shrugged. 'Our mother wanted us to be close. We ain't close, but he's my brother.'

'I think,' she ventured, softly, 'he reminds you of what part of you is and you do not like it.'

He shot her a quizzical look. 'Clever girl,' he said. 'There ain't no advantage in being a Negro in Texas or anywhere else.'

There was a silence between them. Then she said:

'I hope you never have to make a choice between your brother and that belief.'

'No, ma'am,' he came back at her. 'But that won't arise 'cos you and him will be travelling soon and I'll be getting on with my business.'

She bit her lip. 'There is a grave out back,' she said, surprised at her own audacity. 'It will always remind you of what your mother wanted.'

He turned angrily, faced her full on.

'What gives you—'

His words caught in his throat. His eye had captured a movement out on the plains. There was a tenseness in his eye-muscles and an unwavering intensity in his gaze.

She turned, could see nothing. Then she saw

movement, small black dots against the horizon. They were advancing fast and the dots were shaping into men on horseback.

'Who are they?' she asked, catching her breath, fearing to hear the answer, not saying the word that her brain snarled at her in case saying it helped to make it true.

'Comanche!' He voiced that fear, his gaze shifting back to her, his feature betraying what he was thinking, that they must be coming for her.

Maria's lip started to quiver. She tried to move but her limbs refused to co-operate. To escape from that base existence only to have the threat of recapture was cruelty beyond bearing. Aaron broke into her inertia.

'Get inside! Start putting up the shutters. We can't let them see you.'

He waited until she obeyed, then leapt over the corral fence, grabbed the stallion and led him to the barn. After he'd tethered the horse he ran back outside and barred the stable door. Breathing heavily from his exertions, he hurried towards the house. A glance over his shoulder before he entered told him he'd been right; they were Comanche riders, no mistaking.

Maria had barred the windows. She was standing in the middle of the door, a hand to her mouth, looking like a child. Cursing, Aaron picked up two rifles, gave one to her.

'Damn it!' he said. 'There ain't been Comanches around for six months. Why now, with you here?'

In a small voice, she said: 'You think they know?'

He peeped through the window slot. They were no more than 200 yards away. Two were in buckskin, the other three in blue jackets. As he watched, their leader gave a signal and one of them broke away to circle the hut.

'Can't be sure,' he said. 'Got to act like there's nothing wrong. I'll go out and talk to them. Whatever you do, don't show yourself. Could be they just want to trade.' He hesitated before he added: 'Take a look out of that peep-hole, Maria, see if your recognize any of those bucks.'

She edged tentatively across the floor to the window as though she was crossing a chasm fraught with perils, then put her eye to the slit. In an instant, she drew back again. Her hand went to her bosom and she drew in her breath in sharp bursts.

'It's him, Lone Wolf!' she gasped.

Aaron shook his head disappointedly. He stepped to the door.

'I'll try bluffing them. He's been here before so he knows me. It might work.'

He didn't sound convincing even to himself as, with a last glance at Maria, he opened the door.

'Damn my brother,' he said under his breath as he stepped out. 'He always was trouble for me.'

They were lined up fifteen yards from the cabin. Aaron held the rifle in the crook of his arm. As he walked towards them, the other rider, the one who had broken away, rode back into view, joined the line and spoke to Lone Wolf.

Aaron halted half-way between them and the cabin. He stared into their faces, could read nothing in the grim impassivity with which they regarded him. He noticed Lone Wolf was carrying a rifle strapped to his back, that the others seemed to have only bows and arrows.

'Welcome to the Nokoni,' he said. 'Welcome, Lone Wolf. You have honoured me by coming here to trade.'

'No trade,' Lone Wolf grunted.

Aaron suspected the worst now and tightened his grip on his rifle. He couldn't think of anything to say and the Indians just watched him in silence, as though they had all the time in the world.

'Always we have traded,' Aaron stated eventually. 'What has changed?'

'Two people, a soldier and a woman,' the chief said perfunctorily. 'We followed their tracks here. Where are they, Macleod?'

He didn't hesitate in his lie. 'They were here. Spent the night, rode out this morning.'

Lone Wolf regarded him with contempt. The same contempt showed in his voice.

'Only the soldier with your name rode out.' He pointed to the brave who had just rejoined them. 'Little Dog has seen the tracks. The woman is here. You lie, Macleod!'

There it was. They knew and it was no good him trying to bluff any more. He pointed the rifle and started to back away, his eyes watching for their slightest movement.

'Give her up, Macleod and we will leave you with your life,' Lone Wolf said, edging his horse forward.

Aaron just kept backing. They started to reach for

their weapons and he spun round and sprinted for the cabin, driving his feet into the dirt, expecting an arrow or a bullet in his back at any moment. Two yards off, he dived for the threshold, rolled through the doorway, leapt up and without hesitating, shoved the door shut. He heard a rifle shot behind him, then the dull thud of arrows biting into wood as he pushed the bar into place.

Standing near the window, Maria had her back against the wall, leaning on it as though it was the only thing holding her up. Tears were rolling down her cheeks. He hoped she wasn't going to faint.

'You heard?' he said.

'Yes!'

'Well, they won't get to us in here,' he muttered, forcing himself, for her sake, to sound more optimistic than he felt.

He moved to the other window, peered through the peep-hole, could see nothing out front. He changed his line of sight so that he could view the barn. The door was wide open and they were leading the horses out. Last to emerge was Lone Wolf astride the stallion in which all his hopes were invested. He cursed them to hell as he watched his plans for the future melting away before his eyes. Not for the first time, he wished his brother had not come here and brought these troubles to his door.

Out of sheer frustration, he took aim and fired at one of the Comanches but the angle was difficult and he did no harm. Then all the horses galloped out of the barn, driven by the Indians. They were gone from sight in a moment. A cloud of dust, the remnant of Aaron's fine ambition, whirled in their back trail. Literally, before his eyes, his dreams were turning to dust.

Not for a second did he doubt the Comanches would be back and he shook off his disappointment so he could think straight. He figured they wouldn't be able to take the cabin easily, so all Maria and himself had to do was sit tight. The longer the Indians stayed the more risk they ran; time was on the side of the besieged as long as they kept their nerve. His brother would be returning in a few hours. Aaron hoped he'd have the savvy to know that something was wrong, to do something. It was all theory, of course, because with Indians you just never knew what their next move might be.

'Keep an eye out,' he told Maria. 'You see anything, you holler out.'

A moment later a fire-arrow arced its way through the air towards the building. Another one followed it, soaring ominously up into the sky like a comet. He couldn't see the Comanche who was responsible, was powerless to do anything about it. But he knew the target was the roof, knew the intention was to burn him out of the cabin.

He looked in Maria's direction. She had obviously seen the fire-arrows because she had turned towards him, was watching him expectantly, as though he might have answers to this new threat. A faint smell of burning drifted past their nostrils. They looked upwards at the cloud of smoke that had infiltrated through the roof and was creeping across the ceiling.

'What can we do?' she said, forlornly. 'We can't

59

stay in here and burn.'

'Soon as it gets too hot in here, we'll make a dash for the barn, give them a volley as we go,' he said, without conviction.

'Even if we make it, they'll just burn the barn!'

'Then we'll dig in.'

'They'll kill you,' she sad, her voice flat. 'But they won't kill me.'

'Might not come to it,' he said, returning to the peep-hole. ' We must hope that this place will burn slow and that my dear brother will be back in time to help us out of this one.'

Minutes passed before Maria said in a quiet voice: 'I have brought you this trouble. You have lost everything because of me.'

In his irritation, he snapped: 'You and my brother! Don't forget him!'

As soon as it was said, he regretted it. He had wanted to hit out at something because he'd lost his horses. She had been an easy target.

'Yes,' she said, hanging her head. 'Bad luck follows me.'

Aaron, ashamed of himself, coloured up.

'Look, I didn't mean that. It's not your fault. I was just being mean, thinking of myself.'

She didn't answer and he didn't have time to dwell on it. Leaving her at her watch post, he went to the back of the room where he kept his ammunition, reloaded his rifle and stuffed his pockets with cartridges. When he turned round again, the door was wide open and she was gone. He rushed to the door but an arrow thumping into the wood a foot from his face drove him back inside. He half-closed the door, leaving a gap to peer through.

She was walking away from the cabin in a slow, stumbling motion, her body rigid, as though every step she took was a masochistic effort of will. Beyond her, the rider was coming in fast straight for her. Aaron saw a chance, raised his rifle, took quick aim at the oncoming horseman and pulled the trigger.

He was too late. The Comanche leaned low in the saddle and the shot whistled aimlessly past him as one arm snaked out to encircle Maria's waist. She was swept up as though she was no weight at all and he couldn't risk another shot for fear of hitting her. Sick with himself for his mean words, he had to watch the Comanche ride off, his triumphant whoop echoing across the plain.

A moment later, Lone Wolf's voice boomed out.

'We leave now, Macleod. Tell the pony soldier I know how they call him. One day our paths will cross.'

Anger and regret eating at him, Aaron had to watch them ride away. He knew he would never have let the woman go, would have fought them to the last. When she'd run out like that, she'd been thinking to save his life, even though returning to them was the last thing on earth she'd wanted to do. It had taken some guts and it made him more ashamed of those words, spoken in a moment of selfishness, which had helped to drive her out.

When they were at a safe distance, he walked out of the smoking cabin. He watched the flames, already feasting voraciously on the roof, start to spread to the walls. He was burning inside himself as he watched those predatory tongues of fire eating away at his home. The barn was aflame, beyond saving, so all he could do was watch the conflagration taking part of his life away. For certain, without the horses, there was nothing left for him here.

6

Jim Macleod had much to think of as he rode the trail back to his brother's place. Fate, call it what you will, had led to that meeting with Red Bill and he figured too many dead men would expect him to avenge their deaths for him to be able to ride away, to forget what the man had done, to his friend Hooker in particular, that bloody day at Fort Pillow. Maybe the war was over. Some said old grievances should be set aside, that a new start was needed. But the massacre wasn't part of war, it was bestiality given free licence. If the Ranger was correct, the flame-haired devil was still killing Negroes whenever he felt like it. For sure, someone had to hold him to account and doing it legally via the Texas Ranger was one way which had appeal.

By the time he was a few miles off the cabin, he had made up his mind to join the Rangers in their planned escapade. He would take Maria to Sweetwater, provide for her there until the business was finished. She'd feel safe in town and she'd gradually adjust to being around people again. Later, they might want to move on, perhaps head out to

California. Whatever, he would see her right as he'd promised.

Such were his thoughts when he saw the smoke on the horizon. When he realized it was coming from the direction of his brother's place, his focus narrowed right down. One word hammered incessantly at his brain. Though he tried to find alternatives, it beat them all aside. *Comanche* was that word.

He rode all out, hell for leather, not sparing his horse. The last half-mile he slowed a little, didn't want to ride straight into a war party. He'd be no use to anyone dead.

As the distance decreased, he saw the smoke billowing around the cabin. There wasn't much left of what had been his mother's last home. Flames were still raging at the barn and it wouldn't last much longer. He recognized the figure sitting on the ground watching the fires as his brother. There was nobody else around. Instantly, he feared for the woman.

Aaron rose as he approached. Jim could sense that he was either embarrassed or in shock. He reined in, climbed down from the horse to front him, knew from his facial expression it wasn't shock, so it must be embarrassment.

'Comanches!' he said. 'They came for you and the girl.'

Jim removed his hat, fingered the brim. 'They got her – took her back?'

'Lone Wolf,' Aaron said, nodding. 'He came here with five of his men. They saw your tracks leading off but knew she was inside.'

Jim narrowed his eyes, gestured at the burning buildings with a sweep of his hat.

'How come you survived, brother. Incredibly generous of them, wasn't it?'

Aaron stared at the ground.' 'They set the cabin alight and she ran out to them. Think she was trying to save my life. Once they had her, they rode off, left me here.'

Jim nodded. It must have taken something for Maria to deliver herself up to those varmints after what she'd been through. He couldn't begin to imagine what she must be feeling now.

'We'll ride double back to town,' he told his brother. 'Then I'll set off after the woman. I made her a promise I'd get her safe and I've let her down. Shouldn't have left her here. I'm sorry you lost all this. Didn't think there was a chance they'd come this way.'

'He knew your name was Macleod,' Aaron said 'Must have associated you and me and that probably helped them.'

They rode double. Neither spoke as they passed the cross which marked their mother's grave but each had his own thoughts.

'I'll be going with you,' Aaron mumbled when they were clear of the place.

'After the Comanches?'

'They took my horses and I want them back. Besides, I liked the woman, want to help her.'

'What else?'

'What do you mean?'

'Something's sticking in your craw. I sensed your

embarrassment back there. Spit it out!'

Aaron hesitated, then came out with it.

'Something I regret I said, about you and her bringing trouble to my door. It might have made her mind up to run out. I'm ashamed of that.'

'She paid for you not wanting me around. Damn you to Hell for that, brother. Damn you to Hell!'

The sight of two men riding double into Sweetwater aroused the citizens' curiosity. Aaron was known in the town and people called out to him asking what had happened. The word Comanche was enough to satisfy their curiosity and explain the riders' dishevelled state.

Their first call was the saloon where Jim bought a bottle of whiskey. The place wasn't busy and they sat at a corner table. They drank the bottle in silence, both contemplating their loss, inwardly cursing their bad luck. The liquid thrown down their throats didn't assuage their melancholy one bit.

The bottle was down to the last slug when Captain Stoddard, the Ranger who had helped Jim, entered the place and, spotting them in the corner, came to their table.

'Mind if I join you,' he asked. Jim pointed at the empty chair.

'Help yourself. It's a free country most of the time.'

The Ranger sat, eyed them coolly. Sensing their sullen mood, he spoke quietly.

'Heard the Comanches gave you trouble.'

'Trouble is an understatement,' Aaron grunted.

'They burned my place down and stole a woman, not to mention my prize horse.'

Stoddard leaned forward. 'You know which band?'

'Lone Wolf and his Nokoni,' Jim told him. 'The woman was Mexican, a runaway I'd picked up on the trail. She was a wife of Lone Wolf's. He came for her, I guess.'

Stoddard nodded as he absorbed the information. Jim knew the Ranger had plans, was contemplating how this news fitted in.

'This man's a Ranger,' Jim told Aaron, slugging down the last of the whiskey. 'He's fixing to go after Lone Wolf. Best we join him if he'll allow.'

'Like I said before, we could use a man like you. Long as you got your own horse and rifle, you'll be welcome.'

'That include me?' Aaron said.

Stoddard's eyes moved over both, like a gambler assessing opponents. 'You two old friends?'

Jim's and Aaron's eyes locked, contesting who would answer the question. Jim smiled a knowing smile in his brother's direction, then spoke.

'We're friends. My handle is Jim Bass. This is Aaron Macleod.'

'How'd you fellers meet up?'

'Slave and master's son,' Jim said, grinning cynically. 'Guess which is which. My mother was his nanny, see. When the family lost the plantation after the war he took care of her.'

'Now you've lost property again,' Stoddard said, addressing Aaron, 'and you're prepared to put yourself at jeopardy to regain the horse.'

67

Aaron eyed him. 'Without the horse, I'm down to nothing. But if it was just the woman, I'd still go. She deserved a better fate.'

Stoddard seemed satisfied. He pushed the chair back and stood up.

'You'll both do. We're camped south of town by the creek. Ride out there when you're fixed and I'll swear you in.'

As he turned to go, Jim called after him.

'Lone Wolf is meeting with Red Bill, isn't he?'

'Nothing's changed,' the Ranger said. 'We still get to kill two bids with one stone.'

When Stoddard had walked away, Aaron turned to Jim.

'You're a damned good liar,' he said with acerbity.

'What?'

'All that about the plantation and all.'

'I waited but I didn't hear you speak out, brother,' Jim told him. 'No sir, you were real backward in coming forward. I guess I just saved you the embarrassment of coming right out and saying we're brothers.'

After they'd bought Aaron a horse and rifle they rode south to find the Rangers' camp. The mood between them had mellowed but there was still that residue of resentment, a barrier to what could have been a true, brotherly relationship. Jim wondered what it was within him that always had to take an opportunity to snipe at Aaron. He figured it was because his brother always seemed ashamed of him.

The Rangers were camped in tents beside a creek overhung with trees. The two brothers rode through the camp towards Stoddard, who was standing outside his own tent, a mug of steaming coffee in his hand. Other men had come out of their tents to watch the newcomers. Jim could see from their appearance that they were an assorted bunch, just as Stoddard had mentioned they were the first time they'd met.

He counted twelve men in all. Some wore grey trousers with a yellow stripe, signifying they were veterans of the Confederate army. Most had the look of men who had seen too much in this world, had become inured to hardship long ago, had possibly ridden the outlaw trail after the disillusionment of the South's defeat in the war. The Rangers had offered a period of amnesty to anyone who wanted to join them. Undoubtedly there were men here who'd taken advantage. Stoddard had indicated he was short of men for this coming exercise, probably hadn't winnowed the wheat from the chaff because he had little choice but to take what he could.

The captain welcomed them and guided them into his own tent where he offered them coffee. After they'd taken the oath and had stars pinned on their chests, they were given blankets and a tent which they were told to pitch near the others. Stoddard said to get a good night's sleep because tomorrow they'd be pulling out and would need all their energy for what lay ahead.

When they stepped outside, Jim could feel the tension amongst the men, was uneasy with the way they were being scrutinized. He could sense disdain and hostility from one group in particular. One of them, a man with a twisted mouth and sabre cut traversing his nose from cheek to cheek in a thin, wavy line, stepped in front of them. His yellow hair matched the stripe on his pants and he was wearing two pistols with butts forward. His eyes never touched on Jim but riveted on Aaron. He pointed at the star on his chest.

'You and him joined up now?'

Given the stars, the question was superfluous and Aaron stared at the man circumspectly, as though, like Jim, he sensed trouble bubbling behind that innocuous sounding enquiry.

'We are!'

Yellow hair blew out his cheeks, shook his head, made a noise like a horse snorting air. He turned to the other men who were looking on.

'Didn't think we took in black strays, did you, boys? We fight a war to keep them in their place and here they are riding with us and sharing our camp like it was all for nothing.'

'Let it go, mister,' Aaron said. 'Stoddard needs men and we're all you'll get.'

Yellow hair swung his head back towards him. In his eyes, Jim saw a flash of madness that would recognize little restraint.

'A white man riding with a black feller is something we ain't used to, mister. What kind of man are you?'

Aaron shook his head slowly from side to side in the manner of a man exercising an inner patience.

'Just a feller who knows the war is over and these are new times.'

'Bet the Negro can't shoot straight!' one of Yellow hair's companions chipped in. 'Never saw one that could.'

'Yeah!' another opined. 'I used to have one to clean my guns but he couldn't do that right. Shot his toe clean off. Where'd you pick him up, anyhow?'

Aaron kept calm in face of the verbal barrage designed to provoke him.

'None of your business. You mind yours and I'll mind mine.'

So far, Jim had kept quiet, trying to let the intimidation pass over his head. Yet he could sense an impasse had been reached, that the tension building needed release or likely there'd be violence. Talk was a pointless exercise here because he knew men like these. They had their prejudices which they'd take to the grave. Only a cataclysmic event would change what had been bred into them and set even harder by the bitterness of defeat. He decided to walk away from it now but had only half-turned when Yellow hair, still on the prod, called out.

'Can you shoot, boy? You ride with us, you got to be good. Can't have you shooting white fellers in the back 'cos you get scared.'

The voice and the implication grated on Jim's nerves. He knew his capabilities and responded to the goading in a blur of movement. He spun on his heel and pulled his Colt from his holster. He dropped down to one knee and pointed the barrel at Yellow hair who, surprised by the smooth speed and synchronization, took two faltering backward steps, his hands reaching for the reversed butts of his own weapons but never quite reaching home. He stood there mid-motion, his twisted mouth open wide. His whole world had stopped for that moment, leaving him in a state of suspended animation, all expectations cancelled.

Aaron swung his rifle casually towards the group of watching men who were equally taken by surprise. Jim's draw had been as fast as they'd seen and they were rough men who'd seen their fair share. Their eyes were fixed on Jim now with an anticipation that was palpable. The Negro had been baited and the natural response in their book, now that he had the drop on Yellow hair, would have been to pull the trigger. If you drew on a man, you finished it, or one day he'd likely finish you.

Jim did not meet that expectation. With a smile that did not mirror his suppressed anger, he allowed his eyes to flit over them, assessing and dismissing each the way, a moment ago, they had weighed and dismissed him.

'I guess I can shoot as good as most,' he said so they all could hear.

With a contemptuous glance at the bemused Yellow hair, he swung the Colt towards one of the trees and pulled the trigger four times in rapid succession. Each bullet hit the same protruding branch, making it quiver and finally drop to the ground, a cloud of leaves fluttering slowly to the earth in its wake, confirmation if it was needed, of the accuracy of his aim.

When it was done, he swung the Colt back to Yellow hair. Unbalanced by the turn of events, the man had not moved a muscle, though his face had coloured up in anger and embarrassment

'Only shoot men when it's needed,' Jim said, grimly. 'Saw enough killing in the war to last me a lifetime. Saw enough men on both sides lose their limbs or go insane. Guess for some, though, it wasn't enough. Maybe they got to like it.'

'What's going on here?' Stoddard's voice was stentorian as he strode from his tent.

Jim, his gaze never leaving Yellow hair, slid his Colt back into its holster.

'These fellers asked for evidence I could shoot, so I showed 'em.'

Stoddard looked to Yellow hair. Gradually the man's body, which had been as taut as a snake's before a strike, relaxed and his arms dropped away from his guns.

'That right, Dick?' Stoddard asked.

Yellow hair straightened, stuck out his chest in an attempt to regain his lost dignity.

'Some of us don't like riding with Negroes, Captain,' he whined.

Stoddard gave the long sigh of a man exercising patience. His eyes narrowed into a hard stare that would brook no challenge.

'I've already seen this man in action. He'll do for me, which should be good enough for all of you. We'll need every man jack we can get on this mission. He goes with us.'

The men's eyes dropped and they turned away, evading his eyes, some out of shame, others because right now there was no choice other than to let it go. As they moved off, Stoddard turned to Jim and Aaron.

'I don't like shooting in camp,' he said. 'Come to me if there's a grievance.'

'Do our best,' Aaron said. 'But, if you don't mind me saying, you scraped the barrel with some of those fellers.'

'Needs must,' Stoddard said, a hint of concern in his voice. 'But, if it comes to a fight, I figure I can rely on them.'

'Before and after the fight is what would worry me,' Jim said as they watched him walk back to his tent.

After the fracas, they continued on their way and set up their tent on the fringe of the camp. Darkness was falling so they built a fire and lay beside it. Aaron had the makings so they rolled cigarettes and enjoyed a smoke. Neither had spoken about the trouble while they had been busying themselves. Jim broached it now.

'Appreciate you sticking by me back there,' he said.

Aaron dragged on his cigarette, blew a cloud of smoke.

'They were getting at me as much as you. I hadn't much choice. Guess the tables turned on 'em. Where'd you learn to shoot like that? You never handled a gun when you were back home.'

'Had to learn,' he said. 'I've known some rough times. A friend, name of Hooker, he taught me the basics.'

He could hear a melancholy timbre in his own voice as he spoke his old friend's name. He knew that every time he thought of him, a vision of his gruesome decapitation at Fort Pillow would return to haunt him. He'd been too good a man to die that way.

'This friend,' Aaron enquired. 'He was a runaway?'

Jim shook his head. 'He was a freed slave who'd made money. Taught himself to shoot and joined the Northern army because he thought all Negroes should be free like him. He paid for that generous spirit, putting his people before his own interests.' He knew, as he spoke the words, that they were partly directed at Aaron, his white brother.

'How'd he pay?'

Jim frowned, made a sweeping gesture with his arm which encompassed the camp.

'A man, like the ones we just faced, cut off his head at a place called Fort Pillow.'

Aaron grimaced, said softly: 'And you were there, witnessed it.'

'Close as I am to you,' Jim told him, fighting back the incipient tear at the corner of his eye.

'You escaped?'

'Jumped on a horse and ran. I had luck with me but it deserted most of the others. The Negroes I fought with that day were slaughtered after they laid down their arms under a white flag.' He spat into the fire which hissed back at him like a snake. 'That was your gentlemen of the South for you. That was what you didn't see stuck back there on the plantation with Daddy.'

Aaron stared into the fire. 'We suffered in the end. Thank God all that's over!'

Jim laughed ironically. 'After you saw those men

just now, you think it's over? That's how you want it to be, brother, 'cos it's easier for you. The war gave us the right to be free but it'll be a long day afore they let us stand up straight. Besides, I saw the coward who took Hooker's head off in Sweetwater, lording it large as life. Stoddard stopped me killing him but told me that's who he's after himself, all legal like.'

'He knows where he is?'

'Damn right! He's the feller who's meeting up with Lone Wolf!'

Aaron stroked his jaw thoughtfully. 'Strange how loose ends come together, like it was fate playing games.'

Jim shrugged, rose to his feet and stretched.

'We never did,' he said as he entered the tent.

Later, as they lay in their blankets, Jim said:

'You ever think on having a family, Aaron?'

'Sure I do.'

'Ever think how that might turn out?'

'Meaning?'

'You sure as Hell know what I mean. What if you get a kid same colour as me?'

'Face that if it happened, wouldn't I.'

'Sure you would. Daft question. You're just an old opportunist. What's best for Aaron at the time is what counts. Must be nice and cosy in that little world of yours 'cept when you failed to inherit from our white pappy.'

'Drop it, Jim. I told you I got the horse.'

Jim turned over in his blankets, settled down again.

'Blood is thicker than water is what they say.

Wonder why nobody says it should be thicker than colour.'

'You're my brother, Jim.' Aaron sighed. 'And that counts with me, believe it or not. But that doesn't mean we're glued at the forehead. I make the best of what I am, which you can't understand for some reason.'

'Didn't hear you rush to claim you were my brother today. And back there on the plantation you chose the wrong parent. Ma was the one you should have been with all the time. She was the wronged party, remember.'

'You were the one who left and I was the one who looked after her. Remember!'

'Guilty as charged,' Jim said, his tone contrite. 'That's one thing you got right.'

'Then leave it and let me sleep.'

7

They were up early. When the two brothers emerged from the tent, they could smell coffee burning and bacon frying. Three of the men, who had not involved themselves in the previous evening's confrontation, called them over and offered them some of their grub which they gratefully accepted. Jim was glad that at least these men appeared to be friendly and seemed to distance themselves from the three who had been baiting him.

When the men had eaten the captain called them together for a briefing. After a few initial words about the need to be together, clearly aimed to assuage the hostility of the previous night, he came to the real business.

'Fellers, as most of you know, I have information about a meet between the Comanche, Lone Wolf and Red Bill, their purpose to trade guns, horses, women and children. We have a man with Red Bill and he's given us a precise location for the nefarious gathering.'

'What are we waiting for?' a Ranger exclaimed.

'Precisely,' Stoddard said. 'This is a big opportunity. They're meeting in a canyon in the Sacramento

78

Mountains. Our numbers are low in comparison to the renegades but, if we ride hard the next few days, we can set up an ambush which will negate that disadvantage. We can strike a great blow for law and order in Texas if we do things right. Decent folks all over the territory will be grateful for that.'

'This inside man,' Yellow hair piped up. 'You can trust him?'

'He's one of us,' Stoddard said. 'Tried and trusted.'

'Red Bill's slippy,' Yellow hair opined, loudly. 'Your man had better be right. Where exactly is this meeting?'

Stoddard fixed him with his eyes.

'Our man's right but I'll keep the location to myself for now. No need for anyone to know it until we're in the mountains.'

Yellow hair shrugged. 'That's fine by me.'

'Have to be,' Stoddard said and turned to the others. 'Prepare yourselves for some hard riding, men. We got to get to the canyon and in place long before those miscreants arrive, otherwise they'll spot our dust a mile off. Those Comanches have eyes like eagles.'

The group broke up and the men busied themselves preparing for a long ride. Jim and Aaron were saddling up when Stoddard approached them.

'I know you fellers have your own reasons for being here. If there's any chance of getting the women and children out before the shooting starts, I'll try it. But I can't guarantee anything till we see how the land lies.'

'We appreciate that,' Jim said.

When they rode out, Jim noticed Yellow hair staring at him with a supercilious smile. He read it to mean that anything could happen now they were riding into wild country and Jim better watch out because last night wouldn't be forgotten.

Three days later they were riding into the Sacramento Mountains. The journey had been uneventful though the riding had been hard and relentless. As far as they knew, their progress had gone unmarked because they hadn't seen a soul and had cut no tracks. Yet it was a big country and nothing could be taken for granted.

That was why Stoddard led them a circuitous route once they entered the mountains, changing directions several times, enough to confuse his men, never mind anyone trying to follow their progress. On the last day, when their patience was starting to run out, he kept them riding until nightfall, calling a halt in a small canyon where there was a spring and grass for the horses.

When the camp was set up, he called them together. They were expecting to settle for the night but the captain had other ideas. He pointed up the side of the canyon.

'We're going to climb up there tonight,' he said. 'The meeting-place is the next canyon and is set for tomorrow. We need to be in position before they ride in. It'll be a hard climb, boys, but you can get some shut-eye once we're set up.'

No one complained. Whatever else these men

were, most had lived rough on campaigns or as guerillas. They could see the sense in the captain's plan, the element of surprise which could win them the day and decrease the danger to themselves. With the Comanches it was usually the other way round; they were the ones who took you by surprise.

They left the horses tethered near the water and grass and began the climb. Apart from their weapons, all they carried were their canteens filled with water and a blanket strapped across their shoulders which would be of use against the night air while they waited in ambush position.

Two hours later, blowing from the effort, they reached the ridge which divided the two canyons and were able to look down the far side. They had ascended in the shadows, silhouettes of rock formations their only visual guidelines, but this side was illuminated by the moon, making their descent much easier.

Once they were half-way down Stoddard allocated each man his position and told him to wait for his signal before he opened fire. Jim was settled near Aaron and as the night grew colder each was glad of his blanket.

Alone with his thoughts, Jim studied he canyon. It couldn't have been more than 200 yards in length and perhaps eighty yards wide. A narrow stream, like a curled, silver ribbon in the moonlight, cut across its length. While the canyon entrance was narrow, just wide enough for five or six riders abreast, a cliff face rose sheer and forbidding at the far end. The side opposite their position was rocky and offered cover, but anyone hoping to take advantage would have to reach it across the flat bottoms. All in all, he decided, this was a good place to contain unsuspecting enemies who, to choose it in the first place, must be pretty confident their movements would go undetected.

He suddenly shivered and his eyes roamed the grey rocks which seemed to take on a living presence of their own. They seemed to be watching him like stern, sagacious judges absorbing all the follies of the world with an adamantine certitude that eventually everything, however troublesome, will pass and men's lives are nothing in the great scheme of things. They made him remember an old Indian saying that a man's life was nothing more than a buffalo's breath, visible for a moment on a cold winter morn and then gone.

His thoughts brought a sense of isolation and his mind reached out, centred on the woman. He hoped she would be with Lone Wolf, that it would go well for her on the morrow. Red Bill was high on his priority list when the shooting started but he figured the woman's safety was higher. He'd never allowed himself to think of settling these past years, never looked beyond the next day. At first, he'd just felt sorry for Maria, the way one human being should for another abused by life and circumstances. But gradually, almost against his will, he'd found her growing on him. He surprised himself now because he was starting to wonder whether, when the business was done, she would want to remain with him.

Eventually, he drifted off to sleep. In his dreams,

he saw a red-headed man scything through a field of corn but the heads of the corn were human and he was in there in the corn waiting helplessly for his turn to be decapitated. In the distance, at the edge of the field, he could see Aaron watching with a puzzled frown, as though he had no idea what to do.

The distant sound of hoof-beats echoing on rock woke Jim. The sun was risen, its rays seeking out the nooks and crannies in the canyon like the light of righteousness shining in dark places so that evil had nowhere to hide. He took a look around him and could just see the others were mostly awake and aware. Ten yards to his right Aaron was stirring too.

He peered down into the canyon, saw nothing except the rocks and the stream winding lazily on its way. But he could still hear the ominous, relentless progress of those hoof-beats. He tightened his grip on his Winchester and fixed his eyes on the entrance of the canyon from which the sounds came.

The first Indian emerged as though manifesting out of the rocks themselves. The buckskin shirt, the light-blue, high riding-boots and the braided hair all identified him as a Comanche warrior. For a while he just sat near the entrance to the canyon and Jim feared something had aroused his suspicion. Then he turned his horse and disappeared into the defile from which he had appeared. In the moments which followed the Rangers waited tensely, hoping he wasn't reporting back that he'd sensed something wrong in the canyon.

Minutes later their fears proved unfounded.

Other Comanches came into sight, driving with them as fine a bunch of horseflesh as Jim had ever seen. These were clearly the animals they intended trading but Jim could not see Aaron's black amongst them. He looked along at his brother, could see his disappointment.

Other Comanches rode in behind the horses. Jim noticed a group of women and children on foot further back. They were obviously the captives who would be sold as slaves and they were being driven worse than the horses. Amongst them, he saw Maria. He guessed she had been reduced in status because she'd run away. Lone Wolf's recapturing her had been a coup for him, but maybe all he intended was a show of his prowess to compensate for the ignominy after the soldiers had slaughtered his people. Perhaps he no longer wanted or trusted her as his wife. She looked tired and dishevelled like the others but that wasn't too bad all told. Comanches sometimes cut the noses off erring women. Perhaps Lone Wolf intended to sell her too and it was better if all her features remained intact.

Jim eventually spotted the chief riding into the canyon behind his tribesmen. He was sitting astride the black. Jim glanced at Aaron. His brother had seen the horse and looked relieved. All that remained now to complete their satisfaction was for Red Bill to appear. Then all the reasons for being there would be in place.

The Comanches started to make themselves at home. Jim noted that the captive women and children were shepherded away from the main party and left in a cluster of rocks near the canyon entrance. They weren't guarded and he figured they were such a dejected-looking bunch the Indians must think the idea of escape wouldn't enter their sorry heads. In any case where could the go?

Up in the rocks the Rangers were feeling the full force of the sun. They made the best of what shade there was and were glad of their canteens. They had no idea how long they would have to wait until Red Bill and his gang appeared. Patience was the name of the game and three hours later, when he hadn't shown up, it was stretching.

Their restlessness gave way to renewed alertness when, once again, the familiar sound of hoof-beats on rock, this time from shod horses, carried out of the defile to their position. All eyes focused on the entrance as the first comanchero emerged from the shadows into the bright sunlight. A column of fifteen followed him in at an easy canter and the Rangers brightened up at the prospect of some action at last.

Jim searched the column for Red Bill but couldn't make him out. When the men dismounted and greeted the Comanche braves he still could not see their notorious leader. Surely he must have come with his men? He couldn't possibly have the luck to avoid the Rangers when they had the gang dead to rights and were primed to finish them.

'Can't see him, damn it hell!'

The irritated voice belonged to Stoddard who had worked his way close to Jim. His eyes were searching the canyon bottom frantically, like a man looking for a precious piece of gold amongst an excess of dross. His state confirmed Jim's suspicions that, unbelievably, Red Bill wasn't down there where he should be.

With an air of resignation, Jim said:

'He's not there. Don't ask me why but he ain't.'

'The fat one with the sombrero who's talking to Lone Wolf, see him?' Stoddard continued and Jim nodded. 'He's Jake Welsh, his second in command. But he's just small fry.'

'Maybe our man will follow later,' Jim said.

Stoddard gave him a doubtful look. He gazed down into the canyon again, shook his head as he pondered his next move.

'I'll give it a couple of hours,' he stated flatly. 'The men will run out of patience if I wait longer and who can blame them, stuck up here. We'll take them then whether he's appeared or not.'

'It'll be like cutting a rattler's tail off and letting the dangerous part get away,' Jim opined.

'No choice!' Stoddard said, curtly. 'There's fellers down there need curtailing and we got 'em red-handed.'

As the captain made to move away Jim reached out, caught his arm.

'Those prisoners ain't guarded, Captain, and they're near the entrance. If you give me time just before you let loose, maybe I can get them into that defile. Otherwise, they might be used to bargain, or as shields.'

'Nothing spoiling if you try,' Stoddard agreed. 'If they see you, I'll start in. Look for my signal before you make your play.'

'Appreciate that,' Jim said.

When the Ranger had gone, he made his way over to Aaron. He told him what was going to happen, what he intended.

'So the feller who likes to take heads off ain't down there,' Aaron mused. 'Doesn't smell right, does it? You'd almost think that Yellow hair had a premonition when he said he was a slippy customer. Couldn't know he wouldn't turn up, could he?'

'Nothing would surprise me about that varmint. Just watch him.' Jim pursed his lips. 'One of Red's gang will likely sing when this is over.'

'Just be alive to hear the tune,' Aaron said. 'If we get the woman and my horse, it'll be a fair day's work. After that, you can think on Red Bill.'

They shook hands and Jim manoeuvred his way back to his position. As he settled down again, he was wondering at Aaron's display of brotherly concern. He never could figure him entirely, the way he vacillated in his attitude towards him. He wondered whether, if they'd been the same colour, they'd have been like true brothers. It was a cause for regret because sometimes, just sometimes, they were almost fraternal. He put that down to his mother's efforts to keep them together.

8

As the time progressed, Jim kept watching for Stoddard's sign. When it came he started down, keeping low and using the rocks for cover. The descent was easy enough but to cross to the other side of the stream was another matter because of the flat terrain. He'd already worked out it was best to enter the defile where he wouldn't be seen. When he emerged, he was on the right side, no more than a stone's throw from the prisoners and just enough rock cover to get closer.

He took his time, worked his way to a position above the small rock circle which surrounded the captives. Fifty yards further down, he could see the Comanches and comancheros fraternizing. Whiskey bottles passed frequently between them and he could see it was having an effect. He was glad of that, figuring the booze would distract them enough while he went about his task.

He started down keeping his eyes peeled, then lay flat-bellied on a rock ten yards above the circle, gathering himself for the final push. He felt confident that, having come that far unseen, he could get away with it, but then, in one of those vagaries of fate for which there is no accounting, one of the Comanches, clearly a little the worse for wear, left the party and started to weave a circuitous route towards the prisoners.

Jim froze, hoping the Indian was so steeped in the whiskey he didn't know what he was doing and would turn back before he reached the prisoners. But it wasn't to be. Instead, he came all the way, staggered into the circle like a great, clumsy bear entering a den. Jim watched as the prisoners backed away from him, huddling together, suppliant servants fearing a master's whim.

The Comanche made a dismissive, sweeping gesture with his arm, as though their withdrawal from him was of no consequence because he was lord and master here and their resistance to that fact would be to no avail. He staggered forward again and Maria stepped between him and a blonde girl no more than sixteen years old. Not to be outdone, as though she wasn't there, the brave stretched a massive arm over Maria's shoulder and started to examine the teenager's blonde hair, rubbing it between his fingers, a gleam of fascination lighting up his eyes as when a child makes a new discovery.

Maria stood her ground bravely, even though the Indian was hovering over her, his attention fixed on the younger girl. Using all her strength, she pushed with both hands against his chest but it was a futile effort. The fellow was as immovable as the rock Jim lay upon. All he did was laugh, draw back his arm and strike her a blow which sent her reeling away. Then, his face growing ugly and serious, he reached out and grabbed the girl. She struggled but that arm held her like a vice around her waist and in the end her strength dwindled away, much to the obvious amusement of her tormentor.

Jim watched in a whirl of indecision. He hoped the Comanche would just go away but it was clear that was a forlorn hope. The girl's plight was what finally made his mind up for him and, laying down his rifle, he withdrew his knife from the top of his boot. Feet dancing so lightly across the intervening rocks that they seemed barely to touch them, he leapt towards the circle, aware that, for a moment, he could easily be seen by any of the main party who happened to look that way. His nerves screamed, expecting a Comanche war cry at any moment, but it never came and he landed in the circle of rocks a few feet behind the brave.

He drove himself across those few feet like a man possessed, all his being focused on what he had to do. His left hand clamped over the Comanche's mouth like a vice, stifling his imminent cry. Simultaneously, his right hand, the knife hand, prescribed a wide, sweeping arc until the blade was against the Indian's windpipe. With a savage jerk, he drew the blade across the throat before the Comanche had time to struggle. Jim held the body upright, then slowly lowered the lifeless body to the earth. It had been no more than two seconds' work, grisly but necessary.

Maria was staring at him as though she could not believe her eyes. The blonde girl was shaking with shock. He counted another five prisoners behind them. They were watching him with a vaguely optimistic look, as though they hoped he could be their saviour but dare not show too much enthusiasm in case he turned out to be just another disappointment.

'You came!' Maria gasped, at last.

'There's Rangers with me,' Jim said so they could all hear. 'We need to get out before they start in. You all follow me. We're going out that entrance and we ain't stopping till my say-so.'

There was no argument, no questions. A chance to escape had arisen from nowhere at the moment when all hope seemed to have gone for these people. They had expected to be sold into slavery but now there was hope. The big Negro represented that hope and they would do whatever he said.

From the rocks Stoddard watched Jim lead his party towards the canyon entrance. As soon as they had entered the defile and were out of sight, he signalled to his men to ready themselves. Then he poked his rifle over the rock, took a deep breath and yelled out for those below to lay down their arms or be blown to hell.

In the canyon the Comanche and comancheros stopped their carousing, stared upwards to search out the source of the voice, saw rifles directed down at them. Several tried to run, even tried to scramble up the far side of the canyon but they were cut down like ducks in a shooting-gallery. Most, attuning quickly to the hopelessness of their situation, held up their hands, mouthing curses at the Rangers who had them at their mercy.

Lone Wolf hadn't been drinking. As chief he didn't like his faculties to be impaired because one of the ambitious, younger warriors might take advantage, try to take over his leadership. Thus sober and more quick-thinking than most of the others, he'd dived for cover as soon as he heard Stoddard's commands. It didn't take much thought for him to work out that the game was up. He'd considered that in this wild place his people must be safe. The word betrayal hammered its way into his head. Somehow the men above had found out about the meeting. Yet it didn't matter now who had given them away. All that was important was to try to extricate himself from the situation because, for sure, he could do nothing for the others.

The horses were twenty yards from where he lay, the sleek flanks and fine lines of the big black making it stand out even amongst the surrounding quality. If he could make his way to the remuda without catching a bullet and climb on to its back, Lone Wolf figured he might have a chance. As soon as the thought entered his mind, knowing he didn't have time to deliberate, he grasped at it and started crawling.

In seconds he was in amongst the horses working his way towards the black. Skilfully, he bridled it and, careful to keep its body between himself and those prying eyes above, led it towards the rawhide ropes which confined the herd. With a downward slash of his knife, he cut the rope and vaulted on to the horse's back. Digging his heels in, with wild Comanche yells he drove the horses out, running the black in the middle of the bunch and leaning his body to the side of the animal furthest from the Ranger's guns so that he presented no target at all. It was a manoeuvre he'd practised many times and, like all Comanches, he was more at home on horseback than walking.

Aaron had kept his eyes on the remuda. He was sure Jim had managed to get Maria clear, so one object was accomplished. Once he'd retrieved his horse, he'd consider the main business here finished. As he walked through the camp, past the captured Comanches and comancheros, he could see the big black amongst the other animals. It had all seemed easy so far. In a few days he'd be back on his land and able to start building a herd again, all this forgotten.

Suddenly he was aware of movement in the remuda and his optimism decelerated. Something was disturbing those horses. Then he saw it, a shadow moving amongst them, low and swift, visible only for a moment, gone again in the blink of an eye. Aaron knew it wasn't a trick of his imagination. There was a Comanche in there.

He started to run, bringing his rifle up to his shoulder as he sped across the intervening ground. Foremost in his mind was the black, the thought that nobody was going to rob him of what was rightfully his, not again. He tried to get a bead on that elusive shadow but the growing agitation in the herd and the fact that he was on the run frustrated that possibility and, in any case, he risked spooking the horses if he fired.

He saw the shadow moving through the herd to reach the confining, rawhide ropes. A brown arm reached under a horse's neck and there were two silvery flashes as a knife slashed the ropes. Aaron's gut tightened like twisted elastic. He could read what was going to happen but he still couldn't see his target clearly. It was like watching a blow coming at you in slow motion but with your body paralysed so that you were able to do nothing about it.

Lone Wolf's wild Comanche yells echoed off the canyon walls as, seated on the black, he drove the herd out of the remuda and along the canyon bottom towards the exit. Through the swirling dust, Aaron caught a brief glimpse of his body but his shot was too anxious and missed the Comanche chief. The dust engulfed the chief again and next time it cleared the black was in the middle of the running herd. Lone Wolf was hanging to one side, presenting no target at all except for an arm visible as it held on to the horse's neck.

The Rangers, who had been rounding up the prisoners, saw the wild charge and, in danger of being trampled, hurried clear. Aaron found himself in the path of the running herd and had to run for his life. Frustrated and angry, he could only watch as the horses galloped past him and the last thing he saw was Lone Wolf spring upright on the black and wave in mockery as the defile began to swallow man and horse.

Once again Aaron had been compelled to watch

his dreams disappear, the same perpetrator being responsible. If he'd had a horse, he'd have given chase but the Rangers' mounts had been left in the other canyon. The situation was almost a replica of the one when he'd stared into the horizon as Lone Wolf drove the horses away from his ranch. He cursed his luck.

Jim was hurrying his charges away when he heard the sound of hoofs behind him. His confusion grew. After he'd rescued the prisoners he'd been sure nothing could go wrong, that the Rangers were so well placed with the element of surprise that they must prevail. As the noise of the hoofbeats grew louder, he knew that the whole herd must be running down the canyon and his priority must be to take care of the prisoners, so he ushered them into the sheltering rocks where they would be safe.

He gave Maria his rifle and left them there with reassurances that everything was going to be fine. Then he returned to the main trail alone and climbed on top of an overhanging rock. From his vantage point he could see the herd coming four abreast, long manes drifting behind them like women's hair wild and uncurbed in a wind. Their powerful legs, muscles pulsing, thumped an ominous rhythm, like an army charging fearlessly to the beat of its own tattoo.

The commander driving his army on, Lone Wolf, was the last to emerge astride the black, his hair flowing behind him like the horses' manes, riding so adeptly he seemed fused to the black. On top of the rock, Jim crouched. His mind raced but there wasn't time to deliberate. The horses would be parallel with his position any moment. Once they were past, Lone Wolf would be running free.

Still in a crouch, he fixed his eyes on the chief and concentrated so hard that nothing else existed in the world except the Indian and his horse. When he drew level, Jim launched himself. His whole body felt the impact as bone met bone. Enclosing his arms around the chief, he held on as they both hurtled through the air. Though it was only a second, it seemed an age until both bodies hit the ground. Once again, Jim felt his muscles jar. He was forced to release his adversary and, as he rolled, he had no idea what was happening.

When he came to his feet, Lone Wolf was already facing him, his lips drawn back in a lupine snarl. Two black teeth, like fangs, protruded between those lips. His eyes, wide with murderous intent, locked on to the Negro who had unseated him and thwarted his escape. Everything about him portrayed an atavistic image of brutal, primitive man. To Jim he seemed more wolf than human, befitting the way he was named.

Jim was shaky, but aware enough to see his opponent draw the long knife from his belt. He matched him by drawing his own knife. Like animals indulging in a rite of passage, they circled each other, bodies swaying, eyes alert, searching for a weakness. Nearby, sensing the tension between the men, the black horse pawed the ground and snickered.

Lone Wolf glanced at the horse, his means of

escape if he could finish this business quickly. He came at his enemy in a rush, his knife slashing at Jim's chest, missing the Negro by a fraction as he leaned away. Jim's clumsy, retaliatory thrust missed the Comanche's ribs.

Once again, they faced each other. Jim could sense Lone Wolf's burgeoning confidence. The Indian was a veteran of countless encounters such as this. He'd sensed from that first rush that his opponent was just an unblooded amateur. His expectation of a quick finish to the matter was mirrored in the confident gleam in his eye.

Lone Wolf took the initiative, charged. Jim staggered, managed to grip the knife arm before the blade drew blood. His own feeble thrust was easily thwarted as Lone Wolf's hand curled around his wrist. Their bodies were locked in perfect counterpoise, muscles bulging with the effort. Knowing he couldn't endure much longer, Jim gambled and kicked out at the Comanche's legs. The Indian appeared to lose balance, started to topple. They fell together but Lone Wolf, with practised expertise, twisted so that when they hit the ground Jim was the one underneath. He knew then that the Comanche had fallen deliberately in an attempt to gain the advantage, had succeeded in his aim.

He tried to hold that powerful arm but with slow inevitability it descended towards his heart while Lone Wolf's superior strength easily held his own knife at bay. The Indian was so sure of himself now, he was grinning as he pushed down. As his face loomed larger, Jim's nostrils were assailed with a fetid smell, putrid as a sewer, emanating from between those fangs of teeth.

Jim's strength was waning. Death was no more than a few heartbeats away. Bizarre thoughts raced through his head. Regret for the past, knowledge that he had so much still to do with his life, intermingled. The knife reached a point an inch above his heart, hovered there poised for the final thrust which would extinguish his life, make past and future inconsequential.

The boom seemed to come from far off. He felt Lone Wolf's knife arm weaken, lose its impetus. He stared up into the Comanche's face. A darkness, like a cloud traversing the moon diminishing its brightness, crept into the chief's eyes. His body arched stiffly and, trapped in a moment of time somewhere between this world and the next, he froze. Jim found a reserve of strength, shoved the knife arm away from his heart. Perplexed at the sudden reversal, he watched the Comanche's eyelids slide shut, his mouth close on those inhuman teeth stifling that foul, devil's breath. He pushed at the rigid torso and the chief toppled off him, lay crumpled in the dust.

Maria was standing ten yards off, the rifle against her shoulder pointing at Lone Wolf. Jim climbed to his feet, shuffled towards her. She didn't seem to notice him as she stared at the chief's body. Jim had to wrest the rifle from her.

'You had no choice, Maria,' he said softly, conscious she was in shock.

She turned to him, eyes wide and he placed his arm around her shoulder. Leaning into his chest, she started to sob. When her body eventually stopped heaving, she found her voice.

'My tears aren't for him. I thought he was going to kill you.'

Touched and thankful, he said: 'He was! Another second and he'd have done it. But it's all over now, Maria. It's finished. He can't hurt either of us any more.'

The other prisoners started to appear from the rocks, keeping their distance from the chief's body as though he might resurrect himself at any moment to prolong their fear. Jim called them together, told them they were safe, that the Rangers had things under control so they could go back safely into the canyon. When he'd finished, he walked towards the black, took hold of the reins, talked soothingly to the animal. Maria, meanwhile, took charge of the people, started them back. Jim following behind them with Aaron's precious horse.

9

Back in the canyon, the captured Comanches and comancheros were herded together with five Rangers standing at different points of a circle to guard them. Aaron was talking to Stoddard. It was a few moments before either of them noticed Jim and the returning prisoners.

When he saw them, Aaron ran straight to them. He was clearly brimful with joy. His lips were drawn back into a smile and he looked as though he might break out into song.

'Damn it!' he said. 'Damn it all! I thought I'd never see my horse again.'

'Maria too,' Jim said more soberly, gesturing at the woman.

'Thank the lord on both counts,' Aaron said, his voice and demeanour making it clear he was happy to see her safe too. 'How'd you do it?'

Jim sketched what had happened.

'So Maria is the one you really got to thank,' he concluded. 'She was the one who did for the chief or I'd be in the happy hunting ground instead of him and you wouldn't be seeing your horse again.'

By now Captain Stoddard and other Rangers had joined them. Jim told them Lone Wolf was dead and they were mightily relieved. If the Comanche leader had escaped, the mission and their hard ride would have been considered partly wasted, so they were quick to congratulate the Negro for saving the day.

'Pity Red Bill ain't here, though,' Stoddard said. 'Getting him would have capped it.'

'Any idea where he's crawled to?' Jim asked.

Stoddard indicated one of the men beside him, a small, sharp-featured man with lively eyes whom Jim hadn't seen before.

'Dan here was my spy. He was riding with them but he doesn't know his whereabouts.'

'Red Bill left his second-in-command in charge,' Jake explained. 'He said he had a deal to set up and would join us tomorrow.'

'Almost as if he knew,' Aaron said, thoughtfully. 'Like an animal's sixth sense.'

'Maybe someone did know and told him what to expect,' Jim offered. 'That would be more like it.'

Stoddard shook his head. 'I can't see it that way. We kept our business quiet and why would he let his men ride into a trap?'

'Men like him have no fixed loyalties, Captain,' Jim said.

A thoughtful silence followed, broken when the blonde girl suddenly backed away from the group, pointed a wavering finger along the canyon and put a hand to her mouth. Maria hurried to her, placed a arm around her shoulder and whispered consolingly.

101

'What's the matter with her?' Jim asked. 'Tell her she's nothing to fear.'

The girl started to speak garbled words to Maria which some of them caught. Maria, in turn, stared down the canyon, then turned to the men.

'The *hombre* with the yellow hair. He is one of you?'

Jim followed her gaze. Dick, the fellow who had caused him trouble that first day, was sitting apart from the others lighting up a cigar.

'He's one of us,' Stoddard answered with a puzzled frown. 'He ain't going to do the girl harm. What's got her fired up?'

Maria said, 'Can you bring him here?'

Stoddard studied the girl. Her face looked pale and drawn but she didn't look crazy.

'If it helps her mind,' he said and called out. 'Dick! Dick Best! Come on up here a moment, will you?'

Hearing the order, the man took a last drag on his cigar, nipped the end, put it in his shirt pocket and stood up. He lifted his hat and rifle from the rock where he'd placed them, put the hat on with the brim down low and started up the canyon with the easy gait of a man who hasn't a care in the world.

'Captain?' he said, halting a few yards from where Stoddard and the others were gathered and resting the rifle against his leg.

Jim was watching the blonde girl. Maria was holding her tight but her eyes were full of fear as she stared at Dick Best. Her whole body was recoiling, as though a snake had slid into her path and she feared it would strike at any moment.

The captain looked from his man to Maria, not sure what to do next.

'Ma'am?' he said.

Maria focused on Best. 'Will you take off your hat, please?' she asked him.

Best's lips drew back in a slow smile.

'Always do for the ladies,' he said in a Southern drawl but there was a hint of uncertainty lurking in his tone in spite of the smart answer.

With a sly glance round the group, he removed his hat and stood bareheaded in the sunlight. His blond hair was the colour of corn. Self-consciously, he rubbed the scar across his nose.

'It's him,' the blonde girl shouted hysterically and turned her face away, buried it against Maria's shoulder.

Maria's eyes never left Best's as she hugged the girl. He shuffled his feet and raised his eyebrows, as though there was a mystery here but he had no idea what it could possibly be. Eventually, his eyes broke away from Maria's. Scratching his head, he looked to Stoddard.

'A former conquest, I take it,' he said, grinning. 'I always did drive women mad, Captain.'

Stoddard didn't respond to his attempt at humour. His face remained impassive because he was astute enough to know the girl's reaction was way beyond the norm. She was distressed but he didn't think for a moment she was mad. He hoped there was just something in Best's appearance to cause a mistaken identity here, that it had revived a bad memory in a woman who had been under considerable stress, that

103

his man had played no part in her trepidation other than as a catalyst to bring it back to her. The captain turned from Best to Maria.

'What's going on with her exactly? Do you know?'

Maris sighed, drew in a breath.

'She says this man was with the comancheros when they attacked her family's farm a year ago. He was the one she saw shoot her mother.'

'The girl's crazy!' Best interjected. 'You going to listen to a mad female, Captain?'

Stoddard sliced the air with the edge of his hand, silencing him.

'Let her have her say.' He turned to Maria again. 'She could be mistaken, couldn't she? She's young. A situation like that . . . it could confuse the brain. Did the man have a scar for instance? Seems to me she'd remember that.'

'No scar,' Maria said.

Stoddard frowned. 'There you are then. Couldn't have been him, could it?'

'He had no scar when he arrived at the farm,' Maria followed up, then paused dramatically. 'The girl says her mother gave him that scar with her husband's sword a minute after he shot her man down in cold blood.'

Stoddard's eyes narrowed to slits. He glared at Best. This was turning ugly. The man had claimed the scar was an honourable war wound. Now the captain was being given plenty of cause to doubt his man.

Best pushed back his yellow hair. It was damp with sweat.

'She's hysterical,' he snapped. 'The Comanches have turned her mind. Anybody can see that.'

'Then they've turned mine as well,' Maria averred. 'Like the girl, I have seen you before at a rendezvous with the Comanches. You were with Red Bill at the time.'

Jim was watching Yellow hair closely. His eyes were darting over the terrain looking for a place to run, though there couldn't possibly be one. Meanwhile, a silence had settled on the group as the truth sank in that one of their own was no better than the men they'd just captured. It could only be thus, because the women had no need to lie and the young girl's terror was plain to see. Stoddard, having trouble coming to terms with it, looked dumbfounded.

Jim, more ready to believe than any of them, had edged closer to the accused man. As soon as Best started to raise the rifle which had been leaning harmlessly against his leg, he kicked out at the weapon and sent it spinning away from him. The man's mouth dropped open and he made a step towards it but Jim's own rifle came up and pointed at him.

'No guilt, no fear,' Jim said and affected a smile. 'The truth will always out.'

Dan, the man who had been spying for Stoddard, stepped forward.

'Red Bill mentioned a few times he had a brother, Captain, said he sometimes rode with them, that one day he'd be rejoining him. Maybe this man . . .'

Stoddard sighed, shook off his inertia.

'It's possible, I suppose. Leastways, two eye-witnesses can't be wrong. The women have no need to lie.'

'Strange the Comancheros haven't turned this man in,' Aaron speculated. 'They must be wondering where their leader's run to. If they know this is his brother, they're being mighty restrained aren't they?'

'All these men joined him pretty recent,' Dan said. 'Most of 'em are followers and too stupid to work out that Red Bill's probably had foreknowledge this was going to happen.'

'Why should he betray his own men?' Stoddard wondered.

'Like I told you, think on money and you won't miss,' Jim told him. ' If I was to guess, I'd say he's made a pile and doesn't want to share it. This way he doesn't have to.'

The captain's attention turned back to Best.

'And here's the man who would know where he's run to. What was the arrangement, Dick? You'd join up with me because I was out to get your gang and you figured with a spy in our camp Red would know our movements, keep one step ahead. Going to join your brother later, sit on a big pile, and laugh at me and your own kind too. Was that it, Dick?'

Best spat in the dust. He knew now they had him and gave up any pretence at innocence.

'I ain't saying nothing.'

'Whatever,' Stoddard told him, his face red with anger. 'These ladies have led you up the steps to the gallows and you ain't coming down again.'

'One way you might find out where Red is, Captain,' Jim offered.

'Spit it out, then.'

Jim smiled at Best. 'It's a long way back. Give him to the Comanche prisoners and let them know who he is. Turn a blind eye, Captain. Somewhere on the trail they'll find a way kill him real slow . . . or he can save himself for a hanging by speaking up now about his brother.'

Stoddard, pondering it, eyed Best.

'Guess hanging would be too good for you after what these ladies told us. You got a choice to make, Mister.'

Best shook his head slowly.,

'No, you're bluffing me. You wouldn't put me with those savages. It wouldn't be civilised. You're Rangers.'

'You think any man here would object after what we've heard about you?' Stoddard stated contemptuously. 'Somehow I don't think so.'

There was a pregnant silence. Best shifted uncomfortably as he weighed his choices.

'OK,' he said. 'My brother's in Mexico. He has a place near Paso del Norte.'

'A stone's throw across the Rio Grande from El Paso,' Stoddard mused.

Best gave a twisted smile. 'Yeah! A stone's throw, but it might as well be a hundred miles. You fellers have no jurisdiction 'cross that river.'

'Only applies to Rangers,' Jim said. 'There won't be nothing stopping me once I've resigned. I've got business with your brother.'

Best ignored him. 'I've told you what you wanted,' he told Stoddard. 'Now you keep your end of the bargain.'

'He could be lying, just saying anything to save himself,' Aaron suggested.

'Ask the second-in-command,' Best sneered. 'He's the only one knows about my brother's place and by now he'll have worked out that Bill has dumped him.'

'We'll do that,' Stoddard said.

The captain sent a man to fetch the second-in-command. Once he'd been informed how Red had run out on him, he was only too ready to confirm what Best had said. Hearing it, though, was a source of frustration for the captain. The Rio Grande, as Best had been so happy to point out, marked the limit of his authority and it would be risking too much to take his Rangers across. In any case, he had his prisoners to think of now and those who'd been rescued. That made returning home his priority.

'He'll come back one day and we'll be waiting,' Stoddard told Best, 'and there won't be no brotherly reunion because by then you'll have swung.'

'I meant what I said,' Jim informed Stoddard. 'I'm resigning right now and going after him.'

Stoddard studied the Negro. Jim's face was set stubbornly and the Ranger could see that trying to dissuade him would be no use. Beside, it was a way of acting against the renegade who would be thinking he was home and dry, that he'd been clever enough to deceive the Rangers. Red Bill needed shaking out of his complacency and this man was the means to do it judging by his determined demeanour.

'You aim to bring him back across the border?'

'He won't come,' Jim said.

108

Stoddard nodded agreement, turned to Aaron. 'You going with your friend?'

Aaron hesitated and before he could answer Jim spoke for him.

'No, Captain, he ain't. This is for me to do. It ain't his business, it's mine.'

'Well then, you seem set on it and I ain't going to stop you. Don't suppose I could, anyway. You'd just run if I did, wouldn't you?'

'I would.'

'Then all I can do is wish you luck and ask you to keep any connection with the Rangers out of it.'

'You got my word on that.'

Jim and the captain shook hands. As they parted Dick Best, with a contemptuous toss of his yellow hair, called after him.

'My brother's got too many brains for a Negro to take him.'

Without breaking his stride, Jim called over his shoulder.

'I'll see what's in his brain when I take his head off. Don't suppose I'll find much though.'

It took time for the Rangers to bring their horses across from the canyon where they had left them in order to set up the ambush. There weren't enough mounts to go around which meant the prisoners would have to walk. Captain Stoddard said there was a ranch two days' walk away. He hoped that they would be able to hire more animals there.

While the others fetched the horses, Jim slept, replenishing his energy for his long journey to El

Paso. He woke a little more refreshed, cut out a horse and let it drink from the stream while he filled his canteen.

When he turned, Aaron and Maria were standing behind him. Aaron looked uncomfortable, while Maria was just staring in to his eyes, questions in her own which he couldn't interpret. Then Aaron shuffled and stretched out a hand.

'Want to thank you for getting the black for me and to wish you luck.'

Jim shook his hand perfunctorily. 'No need. Lone Wolf was sitting on your horse. I just unseated him. Maria did the hard bit or I'd be dead and the horse gone.'

'You showed – courage,' Aaron said. 'Your ma would have been proud.'

'Our ma,' Jim corrected him with a spark of anger. 'She was our ma, remember. Is that so hard for you to say, Aaron?'

When Stoddard had asked Aaron if he intended crossing the border with his friend, he'd had a chance to correct him, admit they were brothers but, obviously discomfited, he'd kept silent. Now intentionally or unintentionally, he seemed to Jim to be hedging around their fraternity, as though denial was an automatic, inbuilt response.

'Our ma,' Aaron said, barely above a whisper.

Jim accepted that concession with a shake of his head, turned to Maria, but addressed his brother.

'You'll look after Maria, won't you? Make sure she's all right.'

'Of course,' Aaron said, 'Do you doubt it?'

'Guess I don't.'

Aaron turned, moved off, but hesitantly, as though there was something he still wanted to say but couldn't find words. Maria remained where she was.

'You're coming back, aren't you?' she said in a voice as quiet as a whisper in the wind.

Inside himself, he struggled. 'One time I thought . . .'

Misunderstanding his gist, she lowered her eyes. 'What has changed? Is it because I was Lone Wolf's wife?'

Surprised at her misinterpretation, the thought of how it must hurt her to imagine it that way, his denial was rapid fire.

'No! Not that! Not ever! You deserve better, is all. I'm a drifter, see, with nothing to offer. I haven't any money, no home. What good am I to anyone?'

He dropped his eyes. When he looked up again he saw in hers a softer, knowing look, a wisdom of womanhood. It as though she had access to eternal truths which she could trust without fear, even with confidence, now that he had spoken.

'The heart is everything,' she said, just before she turned away. 'If your heart is right you will come back to me. Don't look at anything but your heart. That's all. Nothing else.'

He watched her walk away and sighed long and deep. There was business to take care of, dangerous business and the slaughtered dead of Fort Pillow to avenge. After that, he would, as Maria had suggested, examine his heart, always providing it was still beating.

*

Two days later the Rangers and their prisoners were a weary-looking bunch as Captain Stoddard called them to a halt. He rose in the stirrups, staring at the horizon, his keen eyes studying vague shapes. He figured that from the general direction, those shapes must be Ben Campbell's place. Ben was known to him. He kept a fine herd of horses. The captain was sure he would accept a promissory note of payment for the horses he required, so his hopes rose as he moved his men on.

His initial feeling of optimism diminished as they travelled. Something was wrong but he couldn't put his finger on it. Eventually, he came close enough to realize those shapes were mere shells, that there was nothing ahead but burnt-out buildings. To one side of what had been the main house, tents were pitched and he could see men in blue moving around. It didn't take much savvy to realize the ranch had been attacked, that a patrol of soldiers had arrived, probably too late.

A young, fresh-faced lieutenant rode out to meet them. After they'd exchanged greetings, the solider explained that the ranch had been attacked by Comanches. As he spoke, his eyes drifted to the Indian prisoners who were bound at the wrist and linked by rawhide rope to each other.

'Lone Wolf's bunch?' he asked distastefully, raising an eyebrow.

'Yes. We picked 'em up about two days ago.'

'They're probably the bunch who wiped out

112

Campbell and his family,' the lieutenant stated. 'Been chasing them myself for a month now. Looks like you did the job for me and caught a few comancheros to boot.'

'Rest assured, they'll all pay,' Stoddard told him. 'Meanwhile, we'll have to bed down here if you've no objection. We were hoping to get extra horses from Campbell but that doesn't look likely now.'

'We've some strays we picked up,' the lieutenant said. 'You can have them. Not enough to go round I'm afraid, but your prisoners could ride double as long as you truss them up real good.'

Stoddard's disappointment lifted. In his experience, the army weren't always so co-operative with Rangers.

'Obliged, Lieutenant.'

'Make yourself at home here,' the soldier told him, gesturing at the shells of the buildings. 'There's a little shelter behind what's left of the walls.'

Stoddard thanked him again and set about organizing the prisoners, bunching the Comanches together in the remains of one building, the comancheros in another. They remained tied and the co-operative lieutenant generously assigned his men to guard them so the weary Rangers could rest up.

Everything seemed to be going well, so Stoddard decided to get some shut-eye himself. Under the eyes of the army guards, the prisoners wouldn't try anything so he could rest easy and restore his depleted energy ready for the morrow.

*

Under guard, Dick Best walked towards the burnt-out building amidst the captive comancheros. With a sense of relief he watched the soldiers escort the Indians into a separate building. Telling Stoddard his brother's whereabouts had at least kept him out of their clutches. He figured it was a long way back and anything could happen. Not until they put the noose round his neck would he believe there was no chance of escape.

Jake Welsh, his brother's half-Mexican second in command, shuffled wearily along beside him. The comancheros knew his identity but he'd managed to persuade them that his brother had sold him out too. Why else did they think he was a prisoner? That created enough doubt for them to leave him alone.

As they entered their temporary prison, Jake turned up his nose.

'This place smells of death,' he said.

Best saw the dead dog, the source of the foul smell. A Comanche arrow protruded from its back. The beast had obviously crawled in here to die. The men gave it a wide berth but Best sat down near it, his back to it, his bound wrists behind his back and close to its body.

Jake was the nearest to him as the men settled. None of them spoke. They just sat in the dust, contemplated what lay ahead for them. It was that way until the evening drew in. On the plains, nights could be cold and before dark one of the soldiers came to distribute blankets amongst them. After that, tired from the long walk, most of them fell asleep, the cacophonous snoring rising to a pitch as the half-moon cast a pale light on the ghost of a building.

Best was not snoring, nor was he anywhere near sleep. Since they'd entered the building, his mind had been working overtime, buoyed up because he'd seen a chance of escape. He'd fixed the position of the guards in his brain, noted where the army corralled their horses. Now the others were asleep, it was time to put his plan into action.

Almost gagging from the foul smell, he edged backwards until he was touching the dog's cadaver with his fingers. Overcoming his revulsion, he felt along the length of the cur's body for the arrow shaft, found it and pulled upwards. As it came free, his spirits rose. So far so good.

He waited until he was sure none of the others had seen his manoeuvre, then, like a contortionist, he wriggled back under his blanket still gripping the arrow. Holding the shaft, he slid it through his palms until he could feel the sharp flint arrowhead between his fingers. Next came the tricky part as he tried to use the head as a saw. Several times it slipped away from the rope but he took his time telling himself he had the whole night to complete the job. At last he gained enough purchase and twisted the arrow into the rope, working the sharp edges against the fibres. His wrists ached from the effort but the rope gave and he freed his hands. A glance at the sleeping Comancheros, their faces pale and corpselike in the moonlight, told him his struggles hadn't been noticed.

It took him no effort to leap over the remnants of

the wall. Using the buildings for cover, he edged towards the corral, came within twenty yards of the horses. He could see the guard leaning against a corral-post now. He was looking out to the prairie, unaware the real danger at that moment was from within.

Best steeled himself. Only twenty yards of open space and the guard stood between him and his freedom. He started to move across the gap, his body tensing, his brain aware these were critical moments because he was in the open now and exposed.

Ten yards from the soldier, he stretched down, slid the arrow from the side of his boot where he'd placed it point uppermost. A horse, sensing his presence, snickered. He flattened himself instantly, belly to the ground, cursing the animal. He was so near, yet so far if that soldier took the horse's warning. But the languorous fellow didn't move.

Best rose to his feet. Abandoning caution, like a night predator hungry for its prey, he sprinted the remaining distance. He stretched his arm out, covered the soldier's mouth. Then, with a sharp thrust, he buried the flint arrowhead into the soldier's jugular and twisted.

Even in the poor light, Best saw the blood spurt. He held the guard upright for a moment then, satisfied the last breath of life had left his body, he lowered him to the ground. Wasting no time, he wriggled under the corral fence.

There were three saddles straddling the fence. He picked one, saddled the best horse he could see and led it out of the gate. There was still no sign of alarm in the camp so he walked the horse into the darkness, only mounted when he knew he was well clear and the hoofbeats would not be heard as he rode away.

It was Aaron who, unable to sleep, found the dead soldier an hour later. He'd gone to check on the black, stumbled over the soldier's body and raised the alarm.

Stoddard's face was as dark as the night when they checked and found it was Dick Best who'd escaped. There was no way the Rangers could chase him; in the dark it would be too hard to track him. In the morning, by which time Best would be well away, they had responsibility for the other prisoners, couldn't leave them. The lieutenant, angry at the murder of one of his men, said he would send soldiers after him at dawn. Stoddard told him politely he didn't think they'd catch him, it would be a waste of time. Best had too much of a start and was comfortable in this terrain so that the likelihood of recapture was low, especially when his incentive was to avoid the rope.

When Aaron and the captain were alone, bemoaning the loss of a prisoner who, because of the heinous nature of the crimes, so richly deserved to be punished, Stoddard said regretfully:

'This puts your friend in more danger, doesn't it?'

The thought had occurred to Aaron. 'You think he'll go to Paso del Norte to warn Red Bill? He'd take that risk after he gave him away?'

'For money, yes! He'll want a share of their haul so he'll find a way to weasel his way into his brother's good books. We'd better pray he doesn't get there before your friend.'

Maria had come up quietly behind them and heard their exchange. Aaron, sensing her presence, turned, but before he could speak she spun on her heels and walked quickly away. He sensed she was upset but let her go. When he and the captain finished their conversation, he started back to his bivouac.

Before he had made ten yards, she appeared in front of him. Though he could not make her eyes out clearly in the dark, he could sense fury emanating from her every pore, knew he was the one at whom she was directing her spleen and felt uncomfortable.

'What kind of a man are you?' Her words were a rapid staccato, unerringly aimed, demanding an answer.

He took a pace back. Notwithstanding she'd shot Lone Wolf in an emergency, Maria had seemed a woman of phlegmatic temperament to him. But right how, she seemed to have transformed into a veritable virago. Taken by surprise, he found himself stretching into the silence for words to meet her challenge.

'What . . . ?'

Maria gave him no breathing space. 'You are aware your brother is in greater danger now and you are going to do nothing. You are going back to your bed, to sleep, when his life will be at risk if that evil man gets to Paso del Norte before he does. They will set a trap for him. This you know!'

'We ain't close. He wouldn't want me—'

'He brought you your precious horse back, didn't he?'

'Indirectly maybe he did but—'

Maria cut him short again. 'There are no excuses, Aaron. He is your brother. He's told me how you have tried to run away from that. Maybe it's time you started to look into yourself. Ask yourself what your mother would have wanted.'

With that she turned away, vanished into the night. He was left standing there, her words about his mother's wishes echoing in his head. Her directness had shaken him. It was true he had always tried to keep Jim at a distance because he didn't figure he'd ever make it in a white man's world with him in tow. But, truth was, in these last few days, he'd come to admire him and when all was said and done, no matter what their past differences were, Jim was his brother. He had nobody of his own kin left except him. Besides, he supposed he owed him for retrieving the horse.

Jim Macleod rode into El Paso sweat-stained and dirty from his long ride. The low adobe buildings were a contrast to the ranch house on the plains with which he was more familiar. That, and the number of Mexicans on the street, wearing their wide-brimmed sombreros, left with the feeling he was entering an alien land where he would have to keep his wits about him.

In the distance, through the gaps between the buildings, he caught glimpses of the Rio Grande and, on the far shore, the Mexican town of Paso del

Norte. Red Bill had chosen to hole up there thinking it made him untouchable. Jim considered complacency could well be his advantage over his enemy. Red would be off balance, a fox in his den, unprepared for anyone to come looking.

He hitched his horse outside the saloon and entered. It was late afternoon and the place was nearly empty. The Mexican behind the bar looked up as he approached, then went back to polishing the bar top with a greasy cloth that seemed designed to dirty it more than clean it.

Jim leaned on the bar, pushed back his hat. The barman stopped polishing, looked at the newcomer and raised bushy eyebrows to form a question.

'Whiskey!' Jim said.

The barman swivelled his ample frame, reached for a bottle and glass and placed them in front of his customer. Then, maintaining his air of bored indifference, he went back to his polishing.

Jim poured himself a shot, slugged it back, licked his lips appreciatively. After a second shot, he could feel the liquid burning in his stomach. Knowing his limitations, he corked the bottle intending to save it for later. He could feel fatigue from his long ride starting to creep over him now. His eyes were heavy. For sure, he was in no state to cross the border and go after Red. To do that, he would have to be alert, all his senses honed.

'You got rooms?' he asked the lugubrious-looking barkeep.

'Sure, we got rooms.'

'Could use one for the night.'

The man shrugged. 'Pay up front, you got one.'

Jim took out his wad. It wasn't much but he was sure he had enough. When the barkeep told him the price he considered it reasonable and paid up.

'Keep the change,' he said.

'*Gracias!*'

The polite rejoinder surprised Jim. Encouraged, he decided to probe a little.

'You know a feller by the name of Red Bill?'

The barman eyed him quizzically. 'I know him.'

'You know where I'd find him?'

'Across the river. He owns the largest house in del Norte. It is the last house as you ride out of the town. But he has land too. I am told he has a modest hacienda. Sometimes he is there.'

'Obliged,' Jim said, surprised at the torrent of information. He was pleased that it confirmed he was definitely on the right track; it was better to ask his questions here in El Paso than over the river.

'There are not many Negroes seen here or in del Norte,' the barman added with a knowing look that suggested he could see trouble brewing but didn't want to say so outright. 'You will attract attention.'

Jim smiled, picked up the bottle.

'My good looks don't help me either,' he said. 'Now if you'll forgive me I'm going to lie down.'

The barkeep pointed to a door at the back of the building.

'Through there. The first room on the right.'

Jim nodded and headed that way. When he was half-way through the door the Mexican called: 'You didn't give me your name, *señor.*'

'You won't need it,' Jim called back, then added with a smile: 'But if it helps just call me Black Bart.'

An hour after Jim Macleod retired for his much needed rest, Dick Best rode straight through El Paso's main street. He hoped the short cuts he had taken through the mountains had enabled him to make time up on the man he was following but had no way of knowing whether he had crossed into Mexico ahead of him. Though tired, he kept on going, crossed the Rio Grande and entered the town of del Norte. Once there, he headed straight for his brother's house, rehearsing what he was going to say to soothe Red's temper and hoping he had beaten the Negro.

The Mexican who answered his knock recognized him as Red's brother and led him along the hall and into the living-room. His brother, immaculately suited, had his back to him and was sitting at a piano playing a tune Dick recognized from their boyhood. As the Mexican crossed the room to inform him of his visit, Dick's eyes roamed. The decor gave the room a striking resemblance to their childhood home, as though his brother was trying to recreate his past here, a past that the war had taken away for ever.

The Mexican whispered something in his ear and Red, ending his playing on a crescendo, stood up and turned to face him. His expression gave nothing away as he scrutinized him.

After what seemed an age, he spoke.

'Did everything go all right?' You look like you just

rode through Hell!'

Dick fingered his scar, a nervous habit when he was unsure of himself, then self-consciously dropped his hand from his face. He wanted to come straight out with it but his fear of his brother stifled that impulse.

'The Rangers got them all,' he mumbled. 'Just the way you planned it.'

Red nodded but his shrewd eyes were assessing his brother. Dick realized he must be filthy from his recent escapades, particularly the effort he'd made to arrive here before the Negro. Red, he could see, was wondering why, if everything had gone well, he was so dishevelled. That apart, he had always seemed to be able to read his young brother's mind, to know when he was being duplicitous or evasive. That knowledge made Dick even more nervous.

Red came closer. There was a burning inquisition in his eyes fit to match his red hair. Dick, discomfited, removed his hat, nervously flicked a hand through his own yellow hair.

'There's more, isn't there, Dick? Something I won't like.'

Dick shuffled, wished now he'd just come out with it, got it over with straightaway. Why had he come back here anyway? But he knew the answer to that even as he asked himself. He wanted his share of the money and was prepared to risk his brother's wrath to have it. End of the day, they were brothers, weren't they?

He shuffled his feet. 'We got a problem.'

Red stared at him from under the hoods of his eyes.

'We?' he said drawing the word out with deliberate emphasis.

Dick thought fast, recalling what he'd rehearsed.

'There was a girl, a Comanche prisoner, recognized me from a raid. So the Rangers put me with the others figuring to take me back and hang me.'

'Don't chew on it! Spit it out!' Red snarled. 'You said we had a problem. You must have escaped so how do we have a problem?'

Dick swallowed. 'They were going to let the Comanches torture me, so . . .' He hesitated, looked away to the corner of the room. 'I told them you were in del Norte. Later, I escaped, came straight here to warn you.'

Hearing it, Bill's pallid complexion suffused with red in a visible manifestation of his anger. He seemed to glow. Even his knuckles showed red.

In trepidation, Dick watched his brother struggle to contain himself. He was truly afraid; he knew his brother's rages and there was one building up. Amazingly though, Bill controlled it. The red face gradually turned a shade paler, simmering, not boiling over.

'Suppose it don't matter too much,' he said. 'Those Rangers can never cross the border. Suppose you knew that when you told them.'

Dick said nothing. His silence betrayed him and his brother frowned, perplexity causing his forehead to wrinkle.

'Damn you! There's more, ain't there.'

'There's more,' Dick muttered, head down. 'Don't get angry with me, Bill.'

In the blink of an eye, Red was gripping him by the shirt-collar and spinning him round. Before he knew it, the younger brother was bent backwards over the piano and Red was squeezing his throat. Just as he thought he was going to black out, the grip eased off. After what seemed an age, the fingers let go completely. Gasping for breath, Dick slid slowly downwards and managed to prop himself up against the piano stool. Above him, Red was hovering, staring at his own two hands stretched in front of him, fingers curled inwards like lobster claws.

'If you were another man,' he rasped. 'Not my brother . . . Now tell me what you've been dancing around since you came in here!'

Dick hauled himself up on to the stool but he was recoiling, unsure whether he could trust his brother's mood.

'I came back,' he muttered, voice desiccated. 'Came to warn you.'

Reptilian eyes swivelled sideways, focused on him. 'Warn me?'

'There's a Negro on his way here. He was a Ranger, but he turned it in to come after you.'

'One Negro, you say. That's all? You sure?'

'Swear it on our mother's grave, Bill.'

'One Negro,' Bill repeated. 'We can take care of one Negro.'

Dick sat up, pushed back his yellow hair. His brother's rage had gone. Emboldened, he said:

'Sure we can. No nigger is gonna cause us problems.'

Behind Red's eyes, he could see his mind working.

'When will he come?'

'Soon, I reckon. I can't have been far ahead.'

'Then we'll prepare a welcome party for the uppity nigger. Have us some fun.'

'You figure a whipping before we kill him – like it used to be.'

'Something like that. I don't want him defiling my house though, so we'll meet him in the local cantina. You wait here while I change.'

On his way out of the room Red said something to the Mexican who had stood silently in the corner during the brothers' confrontation. Without a word the man left the room. Red made to follow but suddenly halted, his back straightening, as though an afterthought had just struck him and it bothered him.

He turned again to his brother.

'There was a Negro tried his luck with me in Sweetwater,' he said, soberly. 'He was a dead man until a Ranger interfered. The Negro had seen me before. You don't think it can be the same?'

Dick shrugged. 'This one did join the Rangers in Sweetwater. But it don't make no difference if it's him. He's going down anyway, ain't he?'

'Sure he is,' Bill said. 'But for a Negro he's a slippy one. He needs watching.'

11

Jim rose refreshed. In spite of his nervousness he was eager to finish his long-standing business. The room he'd slept in was as dingy as they come but, after he'd dressed and opened the shutters, he could see it was a bright, hot day outside. It came to him now, like some kind of omen that, back there, in another existence, when there seemed no end to the fighting, his old friend Hooker often said the sun would shine bright again on the righteous. Well, it was shining today. But the fighting wasn't quite over yet.

He realized he didn't know what day it was. It could have been Sunday for all he knew, and Hooker had been a religious man who wouldn't have liked the idea of a killing on the Lord's day. But Hooker had gone to join his Maker, wasn't here to influence him any more. In any case, if this was a Sunday, Jim figured he would have heard church bells by now.

He gave himself a shake. Why on earth was he concerning himself with trivial musings? His friend was gone for ever. It didn't matter when or where a man like William Gaunt, alias Red Bill died, nor how. As far as Jim was concerned, he had forfeited that choice when he made his bloody pact with the devil. All the ghosts of black troopers slaughtered at Fort Pillow would not gainsay that.

When he'd eaten breakfast, he left the saloon. The fat barman watched him as he went through the door. Jim had the eerie feeling that the man knew he had come for a killing but didn't expect there was any chance he could succeed.

He fetched his horse from the barn, mounted up and set off for Paso del Norte. Once out of town, he kept riding until he hit the river. He paused a moment there, let his eye drift across the expanse of water to the town across the border where he would avenge his former brothers-in-arms or die himself. It was a day he had known would come, sooner or later. When it was over, if he survived, he would be able to live without the feeling that those dead men at Fort Pillow were looking over his shoulder with expectations of him. The past would be resolved and he would be able to look ahead, the nightmare of Fort Pillow expurgated.

Del Norte was not a large town. As he rode in, he could see Mexicans but only an occasional gringo and was aware he must stand out here like a black lamb in a flock of white sheep. For sure men's heads were turning in his direction. Beneath the sombreros, curious eyes were assessing him, wondering about his business here. He figured the chances were, if Red Bill was here, not on his ranch, that his adversary would soon hear about the Negro who had ridden into town. It would be best to get straight to it, find Red before he had a chance to wonder.

He kept riding, passed an empty corral and saw the last house, the one he'd been told was Red's. In keeping with the other buildings, it was a flat-roofed adobe but it was larger and more ostentatious than the rest, the dwelling of a man of wealth. It struck Jim as unfair that a man of low character should be so rich but, then again, since when did wealth reflect character or a man's actions? What goes round comes around, he thought, and I'm coming round again Bill, I'm coming right into your back yard to turn the clock back for you.

He rode past the building, then circled to the rear and tethered his horse. He intended walking in the back door, catching Red unaware. If he needed reminding why he was there, he'd tell him, make sure he knew why he was about to die. Then, he'd give him his chance, man to man, a more generous opportunity than he'd allowed Jim's comrades, though he didn't deserve it. It struck him as fitting that Hooker had taught him his skill with the Colt; it would be as though, when Red finally met his nemesis, his dead friend was a participant.

When he was five yards from the door, it swung open and a Mexican stepped out. Jim, in a reflex action, went for his gun but restrained himself from drawing when he saw the man was unarmed and near seventy years old, his skin parched like an old map. He showed no surprise but just looked at Jim dolefully from eyes which seemed dulled, as though he had known life's trials and expected nothing from it. His white shock of hair combined with his white smock to give him an almost ghostly aspect.

'Red Bill in there?' Jim asked nervously.

'No *señor*, he is not.'

'You know where I'd find him?'

The Mexican looked up at the sun. 'He is in the cantina, *señor*. He is a man likes to drink early.'

The answer disappointed Jim. It would have been so much easier to kill Red in his own home without witnesses around. Still, at least he was in town. The cantina would have to do.

'Why are you here?' he asked the Mexican. 'You work for him?'

'My wife and myself, we look after the house, *señor*.'

Jim nodded thoughtfully. The old man seemed harmless, not the devious sort. He decided he had no reason to lie and there was no reason to doubt him.

'*Gracias*,' he said and turned away.

When he was back on his horse, he noticed the Mexican was still standing where he'd left him, staring in his direction. As he rode past he saw the old fellow cross himself. That seemed an extravagant gesture from a man who had seemed indifferent and it spooked Jim. It was as though the fellow knew what he was intending.

The cantina was a long, high-roofed building. Jim tethered his horse, drew in a deep breath and headed for the entrance. He paused on the threshold, peered over the low-swung doors but couldn't see much. In spite of the bright sunlight outside. the shutters were down, hence the paucity of light in there. What light there was came from oil-lamps. But there were too many corners it wasn't reaching, too many dark corners.

Jim didn't like it, didn't like the idea of walking into a place blind. But he figured that if he had difficulty seeing, it would be the same for Red. Besides, he still had surprise on his side. His enemy would not expect to be baited in his own lair, wouldn't expect anyone to have the audacity to cross the border to go after him. That gave Jim the encouragement to push the doors, step inside and move quickly into the shadows.

Leaning ramrod-straight against the wall, he let his eyes wander round the room. The barman, who apparently hadn't noticed his entrance, was busy cleaning glasses. Jim could barely make out his features in the poor light. More worrying, he couldn't see anyone else. He noticed stairs at the far end and they led up to a gallery which circled the room. The gallery was empty too, nobody up there. In fact, the whole place was so eerily silent he wondered if the old Mexican had made a mistake, or if he had been more cunning than his insouciance suggested; had sent him here on a wild-goose chase while he warned his boss.

He started for the bar, his eyes swivelling, searching out the darker corners of the cantina. In the silence, his nerves jangled like his spurs. The barman apparently couldn't hear, or was ignoring him, because he only looked in his direction when he was right up to him. Jim leaned against the wooden rail, positioning himself so that his vision could encompass most of the room and at the same time he could see the barman from the corner of his eye.

'No customers yet?' he enquired, glancing at the man.

He didn't like the knowing smile his question evoked, the predatory flash of white teeth as a fat face looked into his.

'Only you mister.' The man inclined his head with slow deliberation towards a corner of the room. 'And my good friend over there, of course.'

Jim tensed. His head swung towards the corner while his hand slid down to his holster. Though his eyes strained, they could see nothing in the shadows until a lamp flared into life and, out of the darkness, a shape materialized. Jim gripped his gun butt tighter as he peered into the gloom. There was just enough light now for him to make out a body sitting in a chair but the head was cut off by the shadows. The effect was weird, as though the body was head-less.

'Negroes don't drink in my presence.'

Jim recognized the disembodied voice, didn't need the face which thrust itself forward into the light for confirmation. Red was smiling and Jim knew from the self-satisfaction in the smile that he'd been expected. How that was, he didn't know.

Jim could see Red's hands on the table so he felt no instant danger. Pushing away from the bar, he moved towards him, coming to a halt five yards from the table and positioning himself so he could still watch the smirking barkeep in the background. He was puzzled as to why Red appeared so nonchalant.

'You remember me, Red?'

'Sure I do, boy. All Negroes are the same to me, but you, you got an extra smell about you. Figure you're the feller from Sweetwater joined the Rangers after our little fracas.'

Jim knew then for sure something wasn't right. If Red knew that much it was almost certain he'd been forewarned. But there was no backing away from it now, nowhere to go. He'd have to play it by ear, hope luck was with him.

'You remember why I'm going to kill you, Red?' Jim's voice hissed. 'It's important you know.'

Red leaned further forward, his small eyes widening.

'I remember Fort Pillow. Got good cause to. It was the best day I ever had. The look in those Negroes' eyes just before we killed them was something to behold.'

Jim forced himself to remain cool.

'I'll remember that, Red,' he answered. 'When I stand over you, I'll look into your eyes and remember . . . then I'll take your head off like you did my friend's.'

Red leaned back so his lower face was in the light, the upper in shadow. His raucous laugh echoed around the room.

'Never met a Negro with brains and you ain't no exception, boy. You walk in here all puffed up with your new-found freedom and you think saying is the same as doing.' He leaned forward again, hunched over the table. 'You ain't cottoned on that you were expected here? You that stupid?'

Jim went cold. He'd figured as much. But whatever Red had in mind, he was right here in front of him and he'd go down first.

'And you ain't cottoned on you're going to die regardless,' Jim rasped. 'Let's just quit the talking and get on with it. Stand up and draw, Red!'

Unhurriedly, Red pushed back his chair and stood up, hands clearly in view. He stepped forward into the light.

'Pistol duelling is for white, Southern gentlemen,' he opined. 'Why, it would sully my reputation if I fought a Negro man to man like that.'

As he finished speaking, he raised his right hand. Jim was confused for a moment, didn't see the lasso swinging down from the gallery like a snake. It dropped over his head and shoulders and before he could react, it tightened on his arms, pinioning them. The rope was jerked so violently he lost balance, fell on to the wooden floorboards. Cursing himself for his naïvety, he tried to reach his gun but couldn't move.

Red moved quickly, bent over him and took his guns. He straightened again, stood triumphantly over Jim, then stepped back.

'You and my brother are already acquainted, ain't you?' he said.

Jim heard the sound of boots coming across the wooden floor and swung his head in their direction. Dick Best and two Mexicans were sauntering arrogantly across the room. Best was holding the other end of the lasso. Jim knew now who had forewarned Red and wondered how the man could possibly have escaped from the Rangers. Best stood over him grinning.

'Gonna give you a whupping, boy!'

Jim had no chance to reply. All he saw was Best's boot drawn back. He felt the impact as it drove into his ribs and he was aware of the two Mexicans joining in. He tried to curl up. That didn't help much and it was all he could do to stop from screaming out, adding to their crazed satisfaction. Half-expecting them to go for his head, he covered it with his hands. But evidently they wanted him to be conscious of what they were doing to him, to draw out his agony, since they concentrated all their efforts on his body. Two or three minutes seemed like ten to Jim, the recipient of their savagery. He wondered if they intended to kick him to death.

'That'll do it boys. He ain't in no fit state to bother us now.'

Red's command was his saviour, bringing the beating to an end, except for one last kick which Dick drove into his stomach. In spite of pain, he tried to rise to his knees but the swirling in his head and waves of nausea defeated him. He lay on his back. Helpless, through half-shut eyes, he watched Red's face manifest itself above him. He felt the edge of his enemy's spur against his throat, knew that it was sharp enough to cut his jugular, expected it to happen any second, braced himself for it.

Suddenly Red laughed, withdrew the spur.

'Too easy,' he snapped. 'By tradition we hang niggers, don't we, Dick?'

'Never any other way,' his brother replied. 'Hung ten runaways myself before the war.'

'Besides, anyone else has the idea of visiting me

135

down here unexpected got to be made to think twice. You got to put a show on, boy, so people remember how it ended here.'

'Go to hell!' Jim's voice was a weak croak that even he didn't recognize; it seemed a travesty of his own.

Red laughed. 'We'll be along, but you're going there first, boy.'

He felt himself being hauled to his feet. His spirit wanted to fight but his body, exhausted, tender in every part, wouldn't allow him and he had to concede defeat. Even after he was dragged outside and thrown across a horse, he couldn't find the energy to offer even a token resistance.

Though it was only at walking pace, each step the animal took jolted him. It was a small measure of relief when it stopped and he was dragged off. The two Mexicans held him upright while Red and Dick stood in front of him. He could see they'd brought him to the outskirts of the town and that there was a barn nearby. A crowd had gathered at a respectable distance.

Dick twirled his lasso and threw it upward.. The rope caught on a hook protruding high above the barn's main door and which was used to haul grain up to smaller doors above. Meanwhile one of the Mexicans tied Jim's hands behind his back. Dick formed a noose and, with a smirk, placed it around his neck.

Red, conscious of the curious crowd gathering, turned around and faced it.

'This Negro crossed the border with orders from the Texas Rangers to take me back with him dead or alive.' Timing the pause with the confidence of a born orator, he hesitated. 'What right have the Rangers to interfere down here. If we're not careful, they'll be taking over. Mexico will just be another part of Texas to them, a place where they can come and go as they please.'

There were rumblings of agreement amongst the crowd. He had hit the right note. Cross-border resentment was a festering sore with many of the citizens, some of whom hadn't been above a little cattle-rustling and illegal horse-trading on the wrong side of the river themselves.

Red knew the crowd's character, how it would react to the perceived threat to its security. Besides, he had brought money to the town over the years, bought influence here. Money was what counted in a place where there was constant need, Red knew that too.

'It has always been my custom to hang recalcitrant Negroes,' he continued, his voice stentorian. 'We're gonna hang this one slow so folks across the river think twice 'bout infringing our rights.'

While Red spoke, his brother disappeared inside the barn. He emerged carrying a three-legged stool.

'Stand him on the stool, boys,' Red ordered.

The two Mexicans forced Jim up on to the stool. He was still so weak his resistance was token and was brushed off with ease. His head hung low with the shame of what was happening, the shame of his failure to avenge Hooker, but it snapped upright when Dick jerked the free end of the rope. His chin tilted and his neck stretched in the noose until it couldn't go any higher, until the fibres were burning against his skin and all that was preventing him from hanging was the stool which was only just large enough to support his feet. Unaccustomed to such a position, his neck muscles started to spasm. He felt the back of his throat throb.

'Choice is yours,' Red said, matter-of-factly. 'You can make it easy on yourself by kicking off that stool, or you can linger, try to fight it. Either way, you're going to hang. Me, I hope you fight it. Makes it more interesting that way. We'll even run a book on how long you'll last.'

Jim wanted to answer him but couldn't speak. He couldn't even look down. All he could see was the cloudless sky. Its blue serenity seemed welcoming, as though it was telling him all he had to do was kick off the stool and his soul would soar upwards and that would be the end of pain for ever.

'Ramirez, you organize it so there's a man on guard here. Tell him to fire a shot when the Negro's finished. We'll be in the saloon.'

As though from a great distance, Jim heard Red's last order. A silence settled and he knew his tormentors and the crowd had left him there to die at a time of his own choosing, or when his abused body gave up on him and could no longer maintain its balance on that precarious perch.

He was tempted to end it there and then. What was the point in holding on, enduring more agony. He'd already suffered enough, hadn't he? And there was no way out of this. This was a foreign land. Nobody here knew who he was, so there was no chance of being rescued. The blue above him called out seductively. His legs were aching. Yet, he couldn't do it, couldn't launch himself into that blue eternity. It wasn't in his make-up to give in. Not until he had endured to the limit.

After an age, a Mexican voice came from below. In his condition, he grasped at it, dared to hope someone had come to set him free. He sank back into the abyss. He had forgotten that there was a guard around.

'Hurry up, mister,' the voice whined. 'I'm getting tired. Maybe I should give you a little help, uh?'

Jim felt the stool wobble as the man gave it a shake. He braced himself again. One foot hung in mid-air. Only the toes of the other were on the stool. As he sent up a prayer, he heard a cruel laugh, felt a hand guiding his foot back to its original position.

The voice came again.

'See, mister, I have shown you how easy it is. Hurry up! I want a drink and you are keeping me.'

12

Aaron hadn't known the trail to El Paso. Maria's words had stung him into action and, taking what advice he could beforehand, he'd set off with Captain Stoddard's blessing. Good luck, a couple of chance encounters with cowboys who'd set him in the right direction, and the wonderful animal he was riding had brought him to El Paso not much behind his brother and the escaped prisoner. Man and horse were exhausted as they rode in to the town. Aaron worried that he'd driven his horse too hard, hard enough to break it maybe.

Maria's comments had made him review his life, his attitude to his brother. He saw that there was truth in what she'd said. He'd wanted to deny his black origins, live like the folk who lorded it over the Negroes, like the father who encouraged him but in the end had left him no property except the horse. In contrast, Jim had never warmed to their father, had leaned to their mother. That difference and the different colour of their skins had put a distance between them which should not have been, not between brothers. Many times his mother had expressed the desire they should come closer, like true brothers. He saw how his stubbornness, his arrogance must have been a trial to her, hoped he wasn't going to be too late to make amends.

Plodding through town he hesitated outside the saloon. His horse needed water and he was thirsty himself so he tethered the animal at the water trough and entered the building. The bushy-eyed barman gave him the beer he ordered and took his money.

He poured the drink down his throat, smacked his lips in appreciation and, not wanting to waste time, turned to leave. Before he took a step, something made him turn again and address the barman.

'You seen a black man in here recent?'

'Sure, had one stay here last night.'

'You know where he was headed?'

'Del Norte, *señor*.'

Aaron nodded thoughtfully. The Negro referred to was surely his brother. The fact that he had spent the night here had given Dick Best more time to catch up. That was worrying.

The barman, silent initially, was suddenly loquacious.

'You ask me, the Negro was likely headed for trouble.'

'And why would that be?'

The man's eyes narrowed. There was something in the stranger's tone of voice and he looked at Aaron suspiciously, as though he wished he'd remained uncommunicative. But he knew he'd said too much to retract now.

'He asked about Red Bill. Red is a powerful man

in del Norte and he has no truck with Negroes, hates 'em like the devil. Ask me, that means trouble for the Negro.'

It was no more than Aaron already knew. With a curt nod to the man, he downed his drink and left the establishment. His priority was to cross the border as quickly as he could, so he mounted the black and headed straight out of town.

By the time they reached the river the black was tiring again. Aaron sensed the animal's spirit fighting hard to overcome the work load imposed but he couldn't afford to stop. As they crossed the Rio Grande, the roof tops of del Norte were clearly visible and he was thankful that he'd soon be able to rest the horse, which was so worn out it was down to walking pace.

On the trail into town they passed a gringo heading out. The man was no more than a few feet away and he eyed the black horse quizzically.

'Horse is near done in, feller,' he called out, obviously not one to mind his own business.

Aaron ignored the remark but, after they'd passed, something made him call after the man.

'Quiet in town, is it?'

The man, half-turning, called back, ' 'cept for a hanging, it's as dead as that horse will be if you keep on pushing it.'

Aaron only heard the word hanging. It was enough to set his stomach muscles tightening with a presentiment that he was too late.

'Who they hanging?'

'Just some nigger foolish enough to cross Red Bill.

He strung him up at the big barn south of town.'

As those last syllables faded, Aaron's hopes faded with them. The man had been clear enough; Red Bill had hung a nigger. Only one he knew qualified. Multifarious emotions swirled in his brain. The one that filtered through strongest was the feeling that hanging his brother was the same as doing it to him. The strength of his emotion induced a burning anger in him. His jaw set hard. If they'd killed his brother . . .

Closer to the town, he turned south. The barn the passing rider had referred to was large enough to stand out and was set quite a distance from the main dwellings. A quarter-mile out, Aaron dismounted and walked the tired horse towards it.

All Aaron could focus on as he walked the black towards the barn was the figure hanging at the end of a rope, a stool under his feet. He was vaguely aware of a Mexican in a wide sombrero sitting on the ground, his back leaning against the barn. Part of his brain registered the rifle on the Mex's lap, the machete in his belt, but these were peripheral because his mind was in turmoil. It looked certain he had come too late to save Jim.

As he came to within ten feet, he couldn't see any sign of life. It was his brother hanging and his body was motionless, his neck tilted, his face was looking up to the sky. Aaron was sure he'd arrived too late and stopped in his tracks, a bitter sense of defeat threatening to overwhelm him. His efforts had been for nothing. He'd let Jim down.

'You want to bet how much longer the Negro lasts,

gringo? You want a bet with me, uh?'

As the words were spoken, Aaron dared to hope. He did not look towards the Mex, just riveted his eyes on his brother. He noticed a single movement of the feet on the stool, saw that he was supporting himself on his toes, but only just. A thrill of hope revivified Aaron.

'That horse, he's tired like me,' the Mexican droned. 'For two hours, I guard that Negro.'

Aaron let go of the black's reins. It walked slowly to a water trough, leaned its head wearily forward and started to drink.

'Doesn't look like he needs guarding,' Aaron said, forcing a calm, measured tone. 'He ain't going anywhere.'

'*Sí! Sí!* But there are bets in the cantina. I have to fire a shot when he is finished. Maybe I just kick that stool and help him. He is one stubborn Negro.'

'Maybe you and I should have a little bet. Make it interesting for you.' As he spoke Aaron stepped closer to the Mex.

'What you have in mind, gringo?'

The Mexican never received an answer. In a blur of speed, Aaron's gun was out of its holster. The barrel struck the guard's temple three times in rapid succession. He slumped unconscious before his fingers had even closed around his rifle.

Aaron moved quickly. He ran to the barn door, undid the rope and ran to catch Jim as the slackening of tension caused him to lose balance and topple off the stool.

Cradled in his brother's arms, Jim looked up at his

saviour. A sense of wonder intermingled with the pain in his eyes. His voice was a forced, dry croak.

'What are you – doing here?'

Aaron smiled his relief. There was still life in his brother.

'I owed you for the horse,' he replied. 'Besides, when all's said and done, you're my mother's son.'

Jim's eyes twinkled.' You m . . . ean brother!' he stuttered.

'Yeah, brother!' Aaron grinned. He leaned Jim against the barn door and fetched his canteen from his saddle. He made him drink slowly.

His eyes scanned the town while his brother drank. With luck, they were far enough off for what had happened not to have been observed, but it was an exposed spot. Someone would wander up here soon. The black was too weary to carry one man, never mind two. He supposed he could try to carry Jim away on foot. But how far would they progress before Red Bill ran them down? If he caught up, they would be in the open and too exhausted to put up a fight.

For sure, if they couldn't run, they would have to make a stand here. The odds were against them but a plan started to form in Aaron's mind which, if it worked, would at least have an element of surprise, give them an edge. Much depended on his brother having enough strength to play a part.

'We ain't got much time, Jim,' he said. 'Red Bill is down there in the saloon waiting for the Mex to signal you've croaked. We can't run so we've got to try to fetch him up here and finish it. You up for a fight?'

'My body ain't,' Jim rasped. 'But my spirit is. I've been after Red a long time. Tell me what to do.'

'First off, I need your jacket,' Aaron told him.

'Well, they say brothers should share,' Jim mumbled as he leaned forward and pulled the jacket off.

Red Bill paused, the whiskey glass half-way to his mouth. He was seated in his customary chair in relaxed mode, his feet up on the table, hat tilted backwards when he heard the rifle shot.

'You heard it?' he asked Dick who was sitting opposite him.

'I heard it, loud and clear.'

'Looks like the nigger's finally choked,' Red opined, sliding his time-piece from his top pocket and glancing at it. 'Let's take a walk.'

Dick sniggered. 'Want to see those big eyes bulging, uh?'

Red rose from his chair. 'I'm not like you, Dick. I like to make sure of things.' He scowled as he delivered the rebuke, added: 'That way you live longer, brother.'

Dick pouted, threw back his yellow hair and stood up.

'The nigger's dead.'

They walked the road to the barn side by side. As the distance diminished, they could see the body hanging from the rope, neck leaning to one side, as though the Negro's passage into the next world had surprised him and he was looking at it askance.

'That's one dead nigger, ain't it,' Dick said.

'Sure,' his brother answered.

Red's eyes lit upon the Mex. He was sitting with his back against the water trough, his head hanging and his sombrero pulled down low. His rifle and his machete were propped against the trough.

Dick sneered. 'Lazy greaser's asleep.'

They kept walking until they were ten yards from the rope. Red halted, fixed his eyes on the corpse, letting them travel from head to foot. It was when they focused on the feet that he felt everything wasn't right. The Negro's feet were flat on the stool. He felt himself go cold. The posture wasn't right for a hung Negro, he should have been dangling like a puppet.

Dick followed his gaze and realization dawned. 'His feet! He ain't—'

He never finished the sentence. His mouth remained open as he watched the dead man resurrect himself. As though a puppet-master were pulling strings, the angled neck jerked upright, while the arms, which had been behind the Negro's back, shot forward, two pistons working in perfect unison. The fists were balled and in the fists were guns, the end of the barrels fixing on the brothers with wide-eyed threat, daring them. Neither moved, this sudden reversal taking time to sink in and those black-eyed barrels powerful neutralizers in their own right.

After the initial shock, incongruities leapt out of the picture. The face behind the guns was black but around the eyes circles of white stood out like rings on a skunk's tail; the man had obviously covered his face with mud. His features were different too. Now, close to him, the deceit was obvious. This was a white man, not the Negro, pointing his guns at them.

Red recovered first, stepped away from his brother.

'You'd better be good, mister. There's two of us, one of you. Maybe you'd better give it up, leave while you still can.' He paused. 'Who are you anyway?'

The figure raised an arm, wiped a layer of mud from his face with his sleeve.

'He's one of Stoddard's Rangers. I recognize him now,' Dick said excitedly.

'Former Ranger, feller!'

'He joined up same time as the Negro, Red.'

Red nodded. He didn't like the set-up. He liked the odds to be in his favour.

'Negro lover, eh? Where is the Negro, anyhow?'

'He's in the barn, dead as you intended. The Mex over there is dead too. I killed him.'

Red sighed a measure of relief. There was just one man to deal with, then. His guns were menacing but there was a good chance one of them could drop him.

'What was he to you, that made you ride all the way here?' he asked, genuinely curious. 'He was only a Negro and you go to all that trouble.'

Aaron's voice rang out, stentorian. 'That Negro was my brother!'

Red's disbelief was patent. 'Hell, mister, he wasn't. You're white!'

'Hell, mister,' Aaron echoed sarcastically, 'sometimes that's the way it is. We can't choose. Look at you two – a red squirrel and a yellow prairie-dog.

Who'd have thought it?'

'Enough talk!' Dick said, flushing with temper. 'Let's get to it.'

The two brothers had been steadily edging apart. Now, they blatantly side-stepped further away from one another.

'Mistake talking to us,' Red said. 'Should have pulled those triggers, feller. One of us will kill you.'

Aaron smirked. 'But I wanted my brother to have his chance at you, Red. You owe him plenty.'

Nonplussed, Red frowned. His eyes, like skittish birds, flew everywhere, alighted back on Aaron, asked questions.

'Jim,' Aaron called out. 'You ready?'

There was a movement near the water trough. The Mex lifted his rifle, tilted the sombrero right back,. Instead of the Mex's face, a weary, black one, the face of the Negro they'd hung, stared at the two brothers. His heavy-lidded eyes, struggling against weariness, blinked rapidly as they tried to maintain focus. His rifle wavered in his hands, as though an invisible force was pulling at it.

'So he's alive, 'Red said laughing. 'But I guess we can forget him. The state he's in, he couldn't hit a barn door. Big miscalculation there, feller.'

A silence, pregnant with tension, descended. Those present knew the talking was done, that the time had come for action. Death hovered over them, ready to beat its wings.

Dick went for his gun. Aaron saw the movement, aimed and fired at his chest. The bullet hit him in the heart before he cleared the holster. Like a novice dancer attempting a pirouette, he spun round. Then he went down, blood spurting in a crimson fountain from the hole in his chest.

Aaron had already swivelled his other gun towards Red.

But Red was flat out on the ground, his gun pointing. Aaron took a second too long to register his position. He fired hastily but didn't see the result as Red's bullet bit into his shoulder, knocking him off the stool. His head hit the ground hard, stunning him. As he tried to rise, a black cloud interposed itself between him and the light and he couldn't fight his way through it.

As he was toppling, Aaron had managed that one desultory shot. It hit Red in the back of the leg, handicapping him. Now, dragging his leg behind him, he started to crawl, intending to put a bullet in Aaron's brain and finish it.

When he was close enough, he stretched his arm, placed the barrel of his gun against Aaron's temple. Aaron's eyelids fluttered like a delicate butterfly wings. Red's face loomed out of the light, retreated behind that black cloud, loomed again. The red hair, lit by the sun, was a burning halo framing indistinct features, but amidst his confused thoughts, Aaron knew the red signified danger. As the cold steel pressed against his temple, he sensed he had to move but his body wouldn't respond. Even as he heard the voice, reaching him as though from the end of a long tunnel to pronounce his death sentence, he still couldn't find the strength.

Red was on his knees. He cursed his enemy and his

trigger finger started to flex. At the corner of his vision, somewhere near his shoulder, like a fish's sudden, silvery leap from nowhere, there was a flashing arc of light. Then something sharp and excruciatingly, painful bit into the wrist of the arm holding hi gun, slicing through the flesh until it hit bone. Reflexively, his trigger finger jerked and the gun fired, its boom coinciding with Red's agonized scream. The blow on his wrist diverted his aim and the bullet bit the dust instead of burrowing into Aaron's brain.

Red grabbed his mangled wrist, screamed in pain again as he stared disbelievingly at the gaping wound, the exposed bone. He tried to rise from his knees, not knowing what he was going to do, except he had to do something to stop the waves of pain before he collapsed. A powerful hand on his shoulder pushed him back down and he glanced up to see Jim Macleod towering over him. In his hand a machete dripped with blood, his blood.

It had never been in Red's nature to beg, especially from a Negro. But the pain was unbearable. It overcame any remnants of his pride.

'Help me,' he said. 'I don't want to lose this arm.'

'You forgot,' Jim said.

Red's brow wrinkled in puzzlement.

'What?'

'Fort Pillow!'

Red's memory revolved back to that bloody day. His brow unfurrowed and his mouth opened as a suspicion, a grim foreboding, entered his brain. He held up his bloody wrist, stared at it. Visions of other dismembered bodies, his own handiwork, flashed before him in a phantasmagoric parade. He stared up at the Negro, watched him draw the machete back with slow deliberation. The words Fort Pillow echoed and re-echoed in the labrynthine passages of his brain until the moment the machete descended and removed his head.

The crowd, which had gathered at a respectable distance after the first shots had been fired, let out a collective gasp as Red's head bounced. All his energy expended with that last effort, Jim sank exhausted to his knees. The crowd, coming out of its awestruck inertia, started to close in on him. For a moment, as they formed around him, nobody spoke.

Aaron, who had managed to struggle to his feet, burst through the ranks, stood defiantly beside his brother, holding his wounded shoulder. He addressed the crowd.

'This was a feud going back to the war and it's finished now. Leave us in peace.'

There was a difficult moment. One of the gringos, a close associate of Red's, started to pull his gun. A Mexican restrained him. Then, another Mexican spoke up.

'Sometimes the little people, the poor people, can win.' He pointed at Jim. 'This man was as good as dead but he came back. Let us take it as God's will.'

His words hit a chord. With mutterings of agreement, which left no room for the dissenters to object, the crowd turned as one and started back to the town. Only the two Mexicans who had come to Jim and Aaron's defence remained.

'We will show you a place where you can recover in peace,' one of them said. 'Then it would be better if you leave.'

Aaron pulled Jim to his feet, nodded his gratitude.

'*Gracias, amigos*, we will gladly do just that.'

13

Two weeks later, not completely recovered but much repaired, Jim and Aaron looked down on Sweetwater from a ridge above the town. Aaron was riding the black, Jim a nag they'd bought from their Mexican helpers.

'Think Maria will have given up on us and left?' Jim said.

Aaron glanced at him dismissively.

'That girl wouldn't leave, not until she knew the business was done. You can bet she's still there.'

They urged the horses down the ridge. Neither spoke again until Aaron reined in on the outskirts of the town.

'Something you ought to know,' he said, frowning.

Jim sighed. 'Sounds serious. Get it off your chest if you have to.'

'It was the girl persuaded me to come after you. Made me see it was the right thing. If it hadn't been for her—'

Jim cut him short. 'Point is, you did come and I'm grateful.'

Aaron looked away. 'Guess I was confused. Took me too long to grow up, know my priorities. Must have hurt my mother bad sometimes.'

Jim could see his brother's regret was heartfelt, wanted to salve his conscience.

'You were her son. She could only see the good side, same as she could only see mine. Don't burden yourself, Aaron.'

Aaron nodded slowly, sat there a moment longer, then urged the black forward, Jim following at his side.

Captain Stoddard saw them coming and rushed into the street. His joy that they had returned was evident but the unspoken question was behind his blue eyes even as he greeted them, even as he showed concern for their injuries. Jim satisfied his curiosity.

'Both those varmints are dead,' he stated, without emotion.

'Good,' Stoddard said. 'We took the rest of the gang to the fort and the Comanches are back on the reservation. It's a good day for the Rangers.'

'Maria,' Jim said. 'Where is she?'

The Ranger pointed to the general store.

'She's got a temporary job with old Mr Johnson. Keeps asking me if I've heard anything. She'll be glad you're back. Best you go see her. We'll speak again later.'

They entered the store together. Maria was busy sweeping the floor. When she saw them she dropped her brush, ran to them, embraced each in turn, her eyes lighting up like those of a child who has just been given a present, then darkening with concern when she saw they were injured.

'It's finished?' she asked, looking into Jim's eyes.

'It's finished,' he said.

Old Johnson gave Maria the rest of the day off. Later, when all three ate together in the local restaurant, Maria asked Jim what his plans were.

'Think you know I want to be with you,' he said, a little embarrassed in front of Aaron who just grinned at his discomfiture. 'Like you to think about it. It wouldn't be much of a life with—'

Maria's fingers pressing on his arm stemmed his flow

'It is what I wish too,' she said simply.

Aaron's cough broke the moment.

'If you two have no other plans,' he said, 'I'd like it if you'd stay on at the ranch with me as equal partners.'

Jim looked at Maria. 'Suit you?' he asked.

'Suits me,' she answered, glancing from one to the other.

'Thank you, Aaron. Ma would like that,' Jim said, his eyes fixing on his brother's.

Aaron smiled. 'Then I guess she got her way in the end. What do you say, brother?'

Jim laughed, suddenly thought of Hooker and others who had died at Fort Pillow.

'We're all brothers under the skin,' he said. 'The sooner folks find that out, the better.'